INTERRUPTED LIVES

INTERRUPTED LIVES
▬▬▬▬▬▬ ▼ ▬▬▬▬▬▬

Hood's Texas Brigade

Bob Cheney with Diane Holloway, Ph.D.

Writers Club Press
San Jose New York Lincoln Shanghai

Interrupted Lives
Hood's Texas Brigade

All Rights Reserved © 2000 by Bob Cheney

No part of this book may be reproduced or transmitted in any form or by any means, graphic, electronic, or mechanical, including photocopying, recording, taping, or by any information storage retrieval system, without the permission in writing from the publisher.

Writers Club Press
an imprint of iUniverse.com, Inc.

For information address:
iUniverse.com, Inc.
5220 S 16th, Ste. 200
Lincoln, NE 68512
www.iuniverse.com

ISBN: 0-595-16423-4

Printed in the United States of America

To my best friend and lovely wife, Diane Holloway Cheney; and to my mother, Anne Walker Cheney, who wrote the poem.

FOREWORD

Hood's Texas Brigade was one of the most distinguished fighting units in Lee's Army of Northern Virginia, participating in virtually all of the major battles and campaigns from Eltham's Landing through Appomattox. This book, although a work of fiction, is faithful to the movements of the brigade, including its detachment to Bragg's command and the resultant battle at Chickamauga. Prominent in the book are Hood, Lee, Longstreet, and "Stonewall" Jackson, as well as many lesser but real personalities.

But the book is basically about Caleb Walker, a Texas farm boy who enlists after First Manassas and remains with the Texas Brigade throughout the war. It includes Caleb's companions, most of whom will be killed or wounded; the ribald humor of the enlisted men; Caleb's letter exchanges with his girlfriend Liz; homosexual advances; non-combat related murder; the life and leisure and horror of the common soldier; and the leadership, sometimes inept, often inspiring, of non-coms and officers.

Each chapter opens with an account in the Dallas **Spectator** of the war's progress and problems in all theaters of the war, and the home front and illustrates the typical Southern editor's willingness to criticize as well as praise, without fear of retribution.

Chapter 1

The Dallas **Spectator** Newspaper: August 4, 1861

The first insult to the South was the election of the black Republican Lincoln. Then came the firing on Fort Sumter in April. We Southerners have no choice but to rally to the defense of our way of life. President Davis perhaps put it best in his inaugural speech: "The impartial and enlightened verdict of mankind will vindicate the rectitude of our conduct, and He who knows the hearts of men will judge of the sincerity with which we labored to preserve the Government of our fathers in its spirit." Wasn't it Jefferson himself in The Declaration of Independence who asserted that when any government becomes abusive of the rights of states or their citizens, it is their right and duty to alter or to abolish said government? Being outnumbered as we have been lo these many decades in the House of Representatives, and having lost control of the Executive branch to a man who is clearly hostile to the South (as proven by Fort Sumter), we had no choice but to sever the bonds of Union, bonds which we had adhered to voluntarily with the clear understanding that, like marriage, such a compact might with just cause have to be reluctantly severed.

Now the latest insult—the invasion of our Confederate States of America by the rabble army of Yankee clerks. But a just God smiled on our armies, and the thrust into Virginia was hurled back. All we want is to be left alone, to continue our agrarian way of life. But the Yankees are not likely to be just: other invasions will assuredly follow. So we must be prepared: Our young men must take up arms against a distant and unfeeling foe, just as Washington and others successfully defended their homes and their rights against the British. And like our brave ancestors, we will prevail!

Units have already been raised to defend our soil. Right here in Dallas the Third Texas Cavalry Regiment has been mustered, led by Col. E. B. Greer. This unit has already headed north toward Missouri. Former Texas Ranger Captain Peter Ross has raised a separate company of cavalry locally. Many individuals are raising companies of infantry throughout the state, including our own Cecil Sutphin right here in Dallas. The famous sugar planter, Benjamin Franklin Terry, has organized a cavalry unit, which promises to give the Yankees fits. Terry built the first railroad in Texas.

A just cause is a magnet which attracts brave men.

* * *

The day was hot and cloudless, with little movement of the air. The sun was approaching its apogee. A dust devil danced lazily in the middle distance.

An intervening row of green cotton separated the two figures wielding their hoes against the compliant weeds. For many minutes, neither broke the rhythmic pattern of taking a short step forward with the left foot, chopping a weed or two, then advancing the right foot. Then the taller and frailer of the two stopped and looked toward the house.

"Here comes Poppa, and he's got a man with him."

The other removed his floppy hat and wiped his forehead with a sleeve. "Who is that, Jamie? I never seen him before."

"I cain't tell. But he looks like a city man the way he's dressed. You want a drink a water?"

"Naw. I think Poppa's got some buttermilk with him."

The men approached briskly, the heat notwithstanding. The overweight city man was perspiring and wiping his face with a kerchief, while the farmer was carrying a large crock, which made his gait ungainly as he negotiated the rows of cotton.

"Boys, this here is Mr. Sutphin from Dallas. This is my oldest boy Caleb, and my second boy James."

Handshakes and howdies were exchanged.

"Mr. Sutphin is…oh, here, you boys take a pull on this buttermilk. Yer Momma and sister jist made it up and it's fresh and cool. Kindly hot out here, ain't it?"

"Yessir." They took turns at the crock.

"Boys, Mr. Sutphin is goin' around the county organizing a…uh…why don't you tell the boys what yer binness is, Mr. Sutphin? You kin do a better job of it than I can."

"Certainly, Mr. Walker. But I wonder if maybe we couldn't find some shade to talk in? These hard-workin' boys look like they could stand some rest while they enjoy their buttermilk."

A large tree some 30 yards away was tacitly agreed upon, and the four of them repaired there with the two adults in the van. The boys and Mr. Sutphin sat while Mr. Walker squatted.

"I'm sure that you boys know that there is a war on. That the Yankees have invaded the Confederacy and tried to capture Richmond." Both boys nodded thoughtfully. "We've beaten them off so far, but most everbody agrees they'll be back. And when they do come at us again, we have to have some good men ready and waitin'. What I am doing is, I'm going around the county to sign up men and boys to go off and fight for the South, to defend our way of life against the thievin' Yankee peddlers and abolitionists. I've gotten a real good response so far; why, just this morning the two Sammons boys from just east of here signed up. And we have probably 55 or 60 from the county as a whole. What we're shootin' for is a company from this county. A company is roughly a hundred men, as I understand it. You'll get paid a bounty for signing, fifty dollars. And, oh, I'll be the company captain, so you boys will be under me if you sign up. And I'll take real good care of you boys and see that you get fed properly, and we'll go up there and whip them Yankees good and proper and make Texas real proud of us.

"You may know that a few weeks ago Captain Ross of the Texas Rangers recruited a company of cavalry from around here. I assume you boys didn't have no interest in bein' aboard a horse all day and half the night."

They chuckled. "Nosir."

Mr. Walker cleared his throat. "Now Mr. Sutphin, there ain't no question atall about James a-goin'. James ain't but fourteen. I know he may look older because he's tall, taller than Caleb. But he's jist fourteen."

"Mr. Walker, we don't want any boys that young. James needs to stay here and help you and your family with the farm. How old are you, is it Caleb?"

"Yessir. I'm nineteen."

"Caleb, how would you feel about going in the army to fight for Texas?"

Caleb looked at his father. His blue eyes were serious, almost pleading. "Poppa, what do you think I ought to do?"

Mr. Walker stood up and took off his hat, revealing the white brow and bronzed nose and chin of the lifelong farmer. He reflected for perhaps a minute before replying. "I never been in no war. Oh, they's been Comanches around here keepin' us skeered fer quite a spell. But I never shot at none ner had none shoot at me. I don't know nothin' much about war. I know folks kin git hurt in war, kilt even. But you kin git hurt or kilt any time, any place. Why, jist last year over at the Beeler place a boy was kilt at a barn-raisin' when somebody let go of a beam and it hit that Thomasson boy smack on the head; you boys recollect that, don't you? And Mr. Payne fell off his mule and he cain't move atall these last three year. So anybody kin git kilt or hurt without no war." He was silent and contemplative for another minute.

"Caleb, I think you have got to decide this fer yerself. You're a growed-up man now, nineteen. Whatever you decide, that will suit me."

"What about Momma? Do you think she will let me go?"

"I think yer Momma will feel like I do. Whatever you decide, she'll go along with it. That don't mean she won't miss you. And jist because I think you ought to make up yer own mind, that don't mean I wouldn't miss you, son, because I truly would."

"Poppa, what about the work? What about cotton-pickin' in the fall? Kin you and Jamie do it all?"

"We may have to git yer little brother out here to help. I know he's only nine but he's sturdy. And then there's yer sister. Annie's a good hand, and I won't work her no more'n she kin bear. And we may be able to hire Mr. Sammons' nigger to help."

"Yessir. Quince is a good hand. But with Mr. Sammons' two boys gone, do you think they kin spare Quince?"

"Maybe not, but we'll make do. After all, there *is* a war on, and things jist cain't be the same if'n there's a war on. If you decide to go you mustn't worry about us here at home. I'm satisfied you'll have enough to worry about where you are at."

Caleb turned to his taller but younger brother. "Jamie, what do you think I ought to do?"

James blushed with the three sets of eyes suddenly turned to him. He ran his hand through his reddish hair. "Gosh, Caleb, I jist wisht I could go. Wouldn't the two of us give them Yankees hell?" Then, with the realization that he had committed a verbal indiscretion not only before his father but also a distinguished guest, his blush deepened. But to his astonishment his father laughed, then was joined by Mr. Sutphin and Caleb.

Caleb brushed his blonde hair back from his brow and said, "Poppa, you was talkin' about Indians a while back. What if a bunch of us goes off to fight and them Comanches decides to come at you again? Oughtn't I be here to help?"

"That's possible, son, but I don't believe you should make yer decision on a thing that *might* happen. You should decide to go or not go based on what *is*. And what *is* is a fight between us and the North. I don't want to decide fer you, son, but I would be mighty proud if my boy went off to fight fer his country."

Caleb reflected that just a few months earlier his Country had been the United States of America. Now it was the enemy, and he would be taking up arms on behalf of a new Country called the Confederate States of America. Yet he felt little confusion. To him a nation was really an abstraction; his reality was the farm and his family. If he failed to go, would the Yankees somehow hurt his family, damage the farm? Mr. Sutphin seemed to think so, and he was a smart man, educated. And not only was his father no obstacle to his joining up; he actually seemed to be encouraging it. And God knows the family could certainly use the fifty dollars.

"Then I'll go."

"Excellent!" cried Mr. Sutphin. "I won't know for several days when we will have enough men to get started toward Richmond, but just as soon as I do know I will either come out myself or send word to you, Caleb. Mr. Walker, your son is a fine example of Southern manhood, and I am satisfied that he and all these other Texas boys are going to do themselves proud. Good day to you, sir. Caleb. James." He shook hands all around, then departed toward the house, wiping his neck and face with the kerchief.

"Well, boys, why don't you work about another hour and then come up to the house fer dinner?" He took the now-empty crock and left them.

"Caleb, you're gonna be a hero! I jist wisht I could go too."

Caleb only smiled. Then a sudden thought erased his smile. *What if, when I am off in the army, they find out about my Secret?*

Chapter 2

The Dallas **Spectator,** August 11, 1861

The struggle for Missouri will be intense. The Federals seem intent on denying the majority of its citizens the opportunity to join their brothers in the Confederate States of America. A former captain suddenly become a brigadier general, Nathaniel Lyon, has acted in a high-handed way rarely seen among civilized men. He has illegally imprisoned hundreds of state militia and cold-bloodedly killed dozens of unarmed civilians. The world watches in horror this flagrant behavior.

* * *

The night was hot and cloudy. He could see the house clearly now through the trees, with a light showing dimly in every window. The crickets were chirping as he traversed the last few steps to the porch. The dogs penned up at the side of the house barked unenthusiastically, indicating that they recognized his footfall or his scent. He knocked on the post and called out, "Mr. Wright. It's Caleb."

A grizzled man still chewing the last of his supper came through the open door and extended a hardened hand to his visitor, whom he now joined on the porch. "Hello, Caleb. Unnerstand you're goin' off to the army tomorrow. Heard that at the store t'other day."

"Yessir."

"Well, I think that's a brave thing fer you to do. I know yer Daddy must be right proud a you. I sorta wish I had a boy that could go off and fight, but the Good Lord seen fit to give me only girls. Not that I ain't proud a all my girls, you unnerstand. Margaret has give me two fine grandchildern, and Lizzie and Rachel is making a fine pair a girls. But a man jist would like to have at least one son to carry on his name. We did have the boy, you know, but the fever carried him off when he weren't no more'n a baby."

"Yessir, you know I lost a little brother too; he was between Annie and David."

"Caleb, I know you didn't walk over here to see me. I know you come to see Lizzie." He chuckled.

"Well, I come to see all of y'all, and to say good-bye. But yessir, I s'pose I would sorta like to see Elizabeth."

"Son, I don't hardly know how to put this…well, with you goin' off to the war and all, and don't know how long you'll be gone…well, I jist hope you won't take no advantage a Lizzie. Girls kin be awful soft when somebody is a-fixin' to go away ."

"Oh no sir, Mr. Wright, I wouldn't do nothin' that would hurt Elizabeth. She's too fine a girl, and we've knew each other fer so long, as neighbors and in school and all. I think of Elizabeth sorta like a sister, like Annie. You don't have to worry none, sir."

"Thank you, Caleb. That puts my mind easy. You're almost like a son to me, and I thought I could trust you. Let me git Lizzie out here. She ought to be about done with them supper dishes, and if she ain't Rachel and the Missus kin finish up. Lizzie! We've got company."

She joined them on the porch. "It ain't company, it's only Caleb." She was as tall as Caleb, with brown eyes and dark curly ringlets framing a tanned face, for unlike most farm girls Elizabeth worked out of doors without a bonnet or hat. She had pretty, even teeth that, because of her deep tan, looked even whiter when she smiled, which was frequently. Most of her contemporaries teased her about being a Mexican, but Caleb liked her dark look, which contrasted so with his own paleness.

"Hi, Caleb. Heard you're leavin' tomorrow."

"That's right. Come to say good-bye to yer family."

"Go on in and see Maw and Rachel."

He went in to say a brief farewell to Mrs. Wright and the younger girl while Elizabeth stayed on the porch with her father. "Paw, I would like to take a walk with Caleb and spend a few minutes with him by ourselves. No tellin' when I may see him again."

"Sure, gal. I know how close the two a you has been all these years. Why, I guess you all have knowed one another jist about all yer lives, ain't you?"

"Yessir. I can't ever remember a time when I didn't know Caleb. We went all through six years a school together. And livin' so close."

Caleb was back. Elizabeth said, "Paw says it's alright to go for a little walk if you would like to."

"I'd like to. Good-bye, sir." He extended his hand.

"So long, Caleb. You take good care a yourself. And write to us, you hear?"

"Yessir, Mr. Wright, I sure will."

They started off down the path. After a few yards they took each other's hand. A few yards further they stopped, turned toward each other, and kissed passionately.

"I'm gonna miss you, boy."

"And I'm gonna miss you, girl. Who's gonna keep you kissed while I'm gone?"

"Oh, I imagine there'll be a long line at my porch waitin' to take up that chore."

"There better not be or I'll bring my gun back here and shoot me some rascals."

They both laughed softly, then kissed again and again.

"Let's git a little futher away from your house. The sound kin carry a awful long ways at night. I feel kinda bad about what I had to tell yer Poppa."

"What do you mean?"

"He ast me not to take no advantage a you jist because I'm goin' away, and I told him I thought a you like my sister."

"Well, I jist hope you don't never kiss yer sister like you kiss me!"

They walked another hundred yards or so, then stopped under a ponderous oak and kissed for several minutes. They heard a familiar sound in the distance. "Is that a coyote or a wolf?"

"I really cain't tell the differnce," Caleb replied.

"Caleb, are you gonna do anything foolish while you're away?"

"Like what?"

"Like be a hero. Or kiss any other girls."

"A course. I'm gonna kiss ever girl between here and Richmond. And then I'm gonna shoot ever Yankee up north and be the toast of the Confederacy."

"Toast of the Confederacy? Where did you ever learn such a high-falutin' expression as *toast* of anything?"

"Why, in school, a course. You was sittin' right there next to me in the back row. What was you thinkin' about when Miz Stallcup read that to us?"

"When was that?"

"I don't exactly remember when, but prob'ly our last year."

"Durn, that was about six or seven years ago, Caleb. You sure do have a good memory."

"I know that I'll remember exactly what you look like, and all we have ever said to one another, and everthing we've ever did together."

She hugged him furiously, and he thought he detected a tiny sniffling.

"Liz, are you cryin'? I've never knew you to cry. Why, you're the toughest person I've ever saw, male or female."

"A course I'm not cryin', goose. It'll take more than you goin' off to the army to make me cry."

"Then how come I kin feel tears on yer cheeks?"

Their kisses became more heated. His hand went up her skirt. "You don't have no drawers on!"

"I thought you might come over and we might git to take a walk."

As they continued to kiss their breathing became more labored. He removed his suspenders from his shoulders and unbuttoned his trousers, which fell to his ankles. Again he put his hand up her skirt. She was wet, as always. She put him in, and he placed one hand behind her buttocks, the other in the small of her back, and he began to rhythmically pump her.

"Kin we lay down this time?" he said breathlessly.

"You know I'm afraid a snakes. Jist don't fergit to pull it out in time."

Chapter 3

The Dallas **Spectator,** August 18, 1861

Companies continue to be raised all over Texas: in Marshall, Galveston, Robertson County, Woodville, Anderson County just to name a few. These volunteers will be converging on Houston, where the Confederate government promises to equip them. All of Texas, farmers, merchants, doctors, preachers, lawyers, are enthusiastic in their support for our young men who will without doubt acquit themselves in a manner of which Texans can be proud.

*   *   *

The men and boys, some one hundred of them, were gathered in the square. A makeshift platform had been erected, without a covering, and upon it sat Captain Sutphin, a scattering of local merchants, and a few county officials. One of these latter spoke to the recruits and the townspeople, who outnumbered the soldiers at least four to one.

"It's an honor for me to be able to address the second group of our brave soldiers about to go off and fight for the South. I am proud to announce that the county has purchased enough food and supplies to get the company to Houston where I understand the Confederate government will take responsibility for your needs. We have bought flour, beef, bacon, sugar, salt, and soap, plus wagons and teams to haul these supplies. Also our generous local merchants have furnished what we hope will be enough tents and cooking utensils to get you boys to where you get more from the government. Unfortunately, for some reason I cannot understand, the wagons are not here yet, but they should be at any moment. Now let me turn it over to Captain Sutphin. The county is losing a good lawyer but we are confident we are going to gain a great soldier."

Captain Sutphin was perspiring freely under the warm sun and wiped his face and neck frequently as he spoke. "I want to thank the county for the supplies referred to, and our generous merchants for their contributions. When we get to either Houston or New Orleans we will be furnished not only more supplies but also uniforms and I understand firearms. I notice some of you boys brought your own guns, and that's fine. I just hope you have shoes that are good for walkin' because we've got us about a 300 mile walk to the coast. Except I'm ridin' my horse because I'm the captain." There was an appreciative laugh from the townspeople, less from the soldiers.

Then a lady presented a home-made flag to Captain Sutphin, and the recruits filed off toward the south, to the good-byes of handkerchief-waving ladies and girls, the cheers of hat-tossing men and boys, and the barking of half the town's dogs. Their personal baggage was carried on three wagons furnished by Captain Sutphin.

It soon became obvious that many of the soldiers were unaccustomed to walking in the hot sun, and straggling became an immediate problem. There were frequent stops for drinks of water from canteens. (Some of the canteens seemed to contain other, stronger, liquids.) The captain rode to the rear of the lengthening column often, exhorting his charges to "Close it up!" After a couple of hours he became exasperated and shouted, "Dammit, boys, you ain't even carryin' a pack and you can't keep up! At this rate we won't get to *Houston* before the war is over, much less Richmond!" Then the tardy supply wagons caught up with them and the slowest of the laggards were allowed to clamber aboard.

He decided to make camp only four miles outside of town. "Boys, I am thinking we have done enough for one day, with the excitement of leaving and all. Find a place for your tents, pair off, and cook yourselves some food. We need to get an early start tomorrow."

No one was sure what to do. Caleb spoke to a large, friendly young man. "Would you like to be my pardner? I think we're s'posed to each git us a half of a tent and put them together to make a two-man tent."

"I'd admire to. My name is Pat McKee."

"Caleb Walker."

With much trial-and-error effort they finally succeeded in assembling their tent, then turned their attention to cooking. Pat offered, "I'll start us a fire if'n you'll git us somethin' to cook in, Caleb."

Caleb fetched a skillet from the utensil wagon, then acquired some bacon from another wagon. Pat's fire was well under way and they cooked the bacon, which turned out to be more that they could eat. They offered to share it with men nearby but found the surfeit of cooked food a common problem, so that much food was simply thrown away.

"Caleb, I thought that was awful nice a the folks in town to give us sich a big send-off, the band a-playin' and all. And the flag the ladies sewed and give to the captain. And the sweets they give all of us. Some a them girls sure did smile at me nice."

"That *was* excitin', Pat. I jist wish my folks could of saw it, but they couldn't leave the farm."

"Has you got a girl, Caleb?"

"Well, sorta. Me and this girl, her name is Liz, we been a-knowin' one another fer a long time. I *guess* she's my girl. She give me a pome fer a goin'-away present."

"She did? Kin I take a look at it?"

"Well, I don't know, Pat. It's kinda private."

"Oh, sure, I unnerstand, Caleb."

There was a commotion at the next tent. "You damn fool, you've let the tent catch on fire!"

"Well I cain't hep it if the wind come up!"

It was the Sammons brothers from near the Walker place. Caleb didn't especially care for either of them. Both Bert and Ben drank, and when tipsy Bert often became belligerent. They seemed to have been drinking now.

Next morning there was a clatter before sunup. "Get up, boys. Rise and shine. Get some fires goin' and get some coffee and bacon down you. We need to put in a good day's walkin'." The captain was way too cheerful for most of the sullen and sleepy men.

The grumbling was general, but Pat and Caleb teamed up much as they had the previous evening, except this time they cooked only enough bacon to satisfy their needs.

"Don't this coffee taste larrupin'?" said a grinning Pat.

"It do, 'specially since the captain done got us up before God got up." Caleb heard this expression at the store a few weeks earlier and was delighted to be able to use it at last.

Caleb went to urinate. He was standing behind a large pine when he became aware that he was being watched and turned to see that a smiling young man was indeed intent upon observing him. "I'm Henry Dowd. I didn't mean to give you a start. Done pissed myself. Don't look like we're gonna have much privacy, do it?"

"I guess not. I'm Caleb Walker." He extended his hand. "I ain't saw you before. 'Course we only been out the one day."

Henry took Caleb's hand and held it for a long time, looking deeply into Caleb's eyes. "I've saw you. You're kinda hard to miss with that yeller hair."

From then on Henry spent as much time around Caleb as he could. He even asked Caleb to be his tent mate. "I couldn't do that. I wouldn't want to hurt Pat's feelins. Besides, he is so good-natured he puts me in mind of my ol' dog Chalkie back home."

Nevertheless Henry stuck close to Caleb, helping him collect firewood or clear ground for his tent each evening. An observer of Henry's behavior was Bill Tardy, who said to Caleb one day, "You've sure got yerself a shadow with ol' Henry, ain't you, Caleb boy?"

"Well, he sure takes the load off me sometimes. I 'preciate his help."

"Jist wait 'til payday."

"What do you mean by that, Bill?"

"You'll see."

Bill Tardy had first come to Caleb's attention one evening when Caleb was looking for a creek to wash in. Bill was grousing, "That captain don't know shit from apple butter. He ain't once camped us near no water. And he cain't decide if he is a preacher or a prison warden."

"How's that?"

"Some boys got caught stealin' chickens and the farmer marched 'em up to the captain with his scatter gun and the captain says, I heared him myself say, 'I'll hang the next man that steals,' and then damned if the next time one got caught stealin' peaches if the fool captain didn't offer to pay the farmer fer his losses. But the farmer craw-dadded and mumbled somethin' about he guessed he could donate a few peaches to boys as was goin' off to fight fer the South."

"Well, he ain't had no experience at bein' a captain."

"Look, when we go into battle he may ast us to foller him up a hog's ass. I'd like to know that a man has got *some* idee what the hell's goin' on if'n he's got my life in his hands."

Rain seemed to fall more days than not. Not only did the rain slow the march by turning roads into quagmires, it also deepened the men's demoralization by turning the camps into muddy wallows, and making the fires hard to start and maintain. One who seemed unperturbed by the rain was John Martin. "It's the Lord's will. He is putting moisture in the ground for the farmers' next planting."

"He plainly likes farmers better'n he likes soldiers, I vow," cried an exasperated Bill.

John replied, "In His infinite wisdom the Lord is testing us to see if we have the character that will be required of us in battle."

"Bullshit," was Bill's answer.

John was cheerful, almost as much as Pat, thought Caleb. He was the first to volunteer for any task. When not working he read his Bible, propped against a tree or a wagon wheel.

The company's progress south became slightly smoother as the days passed, despite the rain and mud, and despite the appearance of sutlers with their wagonloads of goods to tempt the recruits at inflated prices. For one thing, getting camp set up in the evening became more routine. A site was selected, the men fell out to choose individual tent locations, slit trenches were dug for toilet purposes, fires were started for evening meals, all virtually automatically, with little required in the way of supervision. Sometimes they camped in a pecan grove, and the men excitedly harvested and ate this bonanza. Some of the new soldiers were like carefree schoolboys out on a protracted holiday, with no need to bathe or use good table manners. Others, however, like Caleb, were appalled at the lack of privacy, especially when defecating or even urinating.

Every time the company passed through a town or a community the citizens turned out to cheer or encourage or at least gawk at them. Often they were given peaches or cookies or flowers or jars of something to drink. Most of the soldiers were exhilarated; Tolly Johnson was not. "Ever time I see a purty girl she reminds me a my sweet Sally back home."

Caleb asked, "Who's Sally, Tolly?"

"My wife."

"Why'd you join up and go off and leave yer wife if you're missin' her already, fool?" Bill asked.

"I don't know. It jist seemed like a good idee at the time. Everbody was talkin' about fightin' Yankees and savin' the South and I guess I jist got caught up in it."

"What did yer wife think about you joinin' up and leavin' her?" from John.

"She didn't say much. Sal has always, ever since I've knew her, even before we got married up, kinda let me take the lead in everthing. So when the war talk got started and I said somethin' about joinin', she didn't really say nothin'. So I done it. Now I'm wonderin' if Sal kin take care of herself with me gone."

"She'll be fine, Tolly," said the optimistic Pat.

*   *   *

The further south they went the flatter the land became and the more slaves they saw. Most of them were working in gangs, with a mounted white overseer or an unmounted black driver urging them on. Sometimes they were lashed. Most of the soldiers, being like Caleb from areas where small farms were the rule and slaves rare, were quiet and subdued when they witnessed these punishments. But they said little. Only Henry seemed not to disapprove.

As they neared Houston they began to encounter other companies of volunteers headed for the coast. Rumors spread that they were to ride a railroad soon. "I don't believe there is no railroads in Texas," declared Bill. But he was wrong; they rode a train from Harrisburg to Houston. Bill, Caleb, Tolly, and Pat were put on a flat car. As the train picked up speed Pat's hat blew off. Bill, who had been subdued because his prophecy had been proved wrong, laughed uproariously.

*   *   *

At Houston they were issued gray uniforms and shoes. They slept in a warehouse, Henry getting as close to Caleb as possible. Here they were joined by a company from Galveston and nearby counties composed entirely of French Catholics, all descended from the dispersed armies of Napoleon. With them was a priest of whom they were inordinately proud. "He has built churches, infirmaries, and orphanages all over Texas, and now he is going to war with us. How can we come to harm with Father Chambodut with us?"

From Houston they took a train to Beaumont, then were marched into Louisiana. None of them had ever seen so much water. "Has it jist flooded here?" Bill inquired of a local.

The reply was in an accent they could barely comprehend. "Naw, she alway lak dis, boo-coo wautah."

The mosquitoes were numerous and persistent. "I've saw big skeeters before, but none as big as buzzards like these Goddamn things!" cried an irritated Bill. And snakes were a constant source of danger, mostly water moccasins, occasionally rattlesnakes or copperheads or even coral snakes. But the most unusual inhabitants of the swamps were the alligators. It was hard to know who feared them most, Bill or Pat. Every time one of the hideous creatures showed itself Bill would jump and scream, "Shit, there's another one!" Pat's favored reaction was to shudder and recoil, rolling his eyes up in his head. Predictably, John referred to them as "God's creatures." And Bill would reply, "God musta been in a hell of a bad temper when he made them ugly Goddamn things."

As their progress through the swamps slowed to a crawl, many of the men discarded their equipment, even their clothing, undergarments first, since many of these farm boys were unaccustomed to undergarments anyhow. Not Bill. "These damn fools is gonna feel awful Goddamn silly when they walk into the next town nekkid as jaybirds."

And so it was when at last they reached New Orleans. Despite the scraggly appearance of the Texans, the populace received them with wild jubilation, calling them Texicans. Those who were lacking certain articles of clothing were immediately furnished with replacements, most of them ill-fitting.

Caleb could not believe a river could be as wide as the Mississippi was, coming as he did from arid North Texas where the rivers were little more than glorified creeks. "I've heard the Missippi was big, but I didn't have no idee it were *this* big."

At New Orleans they were issued muskets, a gray coat, gray trousers, two butternut shirts, undergarments, a wool hat, blanket, cartridge box, cap box, haversack for food, knapsack for clothing, flannel-covered canteen, tin cups; and every other man was issued a frying pan. Then they were put aboard trains bound for Richmond.

Their progress northward was hindered by frequent changes of trains necessitated by differing gauges of track. Whenever they paused to board other trains the locals showered them with enthusiasm, gifts, and speeches. Many of the men either spent their money on spirits or did not need to, given the generosity of their countrymen.

Ben Sammons seemed to have been drunk at least since leaving New Orleans. Caleb was concerned about his condition, especially when at one railroad change Ben found himself riding on the coupling between two cars. In a remote area of Mississippi, as the train rounded a bend, a frantic shout went up that a man had fallen off the train. It took a mile for this news to reach the engineer and for him to stop the train. Men hurried back to the scene of the mishap to find that Ben Sammons had fallen beneath the wheels of the train and had been cut completely in two. He was taken to the next town and given a hero's burial.

"Don't it seem like a real shame fer Ben to be kilt before he even got to the war?" Pat lamented.

John volunteered, "The evil brew is what done him in."

"What done the dumb bastard in was bein' too damn drunk to stay on the train. At least if he was gonna fall off, he should of fell off away from the wheels," said Bill.

"I go along with Pat," Caleb interjected. "The man joined up to fight Yankees and never got to *see* no Yankee."

"A fool like that, drunk half the time, he mighta shot one a *us*," Bill cried.

"Bill, you ought to of been a missionary," observed Tolly. They laughed.

In Knoxville the inevitable off-loading took place. As they waited for the new train to be brought into the yard, a rumor reached them that a United States flag had been observed flying from a nearby house. Dozens of them rushed to the house. Sure enough, flying from the top of the two-story home was the enemy flag. A delegation of the soldiers went to the door and knocked. The man who answered said that yes, he was aware that the Union flag was flying atop his house and that no, he did not intend to take it down. The conversation grew more heated, and finally it was Henry who shouted, "We're gonna take that Goddamn flag down, and if you try to stop us we're gonna kill you and burn yer Goddamn house to the ground, you Yankee-lovin' son of a bitch!" Caleb could scarcely believe that this was the same person who could be so helpful to him; but he also noted that Henry had been drinking heavily. The soldiers removed the flag.

* * *

As they rolled toward Richmond the fervor of the crowds became more pronounced. The excitement of the Texans mounted. Caleb had mixed emotions. He was excited about getting close to the arena of war. But in his consciousness too was the lurking awareness of his Secret.

Chapter 4

▼

The Dallas **Spectator:** September 1, 1861

President Davis has his government in Richmond assembled and functioning. He has chosen his cabinet officers with an eye both to ability and to geography. His Secretary of State is R. M. T. Hunter of Virginia, recent replacement for Robert Toombs of Georgia, who has bravely decided to lead Georgian troops into battle. The Secretary of the Treasury is South Carolina's Christopher Memminger: Alabama is represented by Leroy Walker as Secretary of War; Secretary of the Navy is Stephen Mallory of Florida; Texas' own John H. Reagan should be an outstanding Postmaster General; and rounding out the cabinet as Attorney General is Louisiana's Judah Benjamin. There is not a man on the list who is not able and experienced. The new government should have unlimited success.

* * *

Richmond was bustling. Government officials, soldiers, businessmen were everywhere. The muddy streets and board sidewalks were jammed day and night as the capital of the new nation pulsated with the activity of a new and optimistic beginning.

The company from Texas, hot, dirty, weary from long traveling, was scarcely noticed in all this boom and hub-bub. Caleb was typical in his reaction. "Boy, this sure is crowded. I never seen so many folks in such a hurry. This town jist may bust."

They were taken outside the city to an encampment that already included several other companies from Texas. To add to the gear already in their possession—muskets, cooking utensils, ponchos—they were issued tents and additional blankets. And they were paid for the first time in crisp Confederate bills.

"Bill, you said wait 'til payday and I would find out somethin' about Henry. Well, we had us a payday and nothin' happened about Henry."

"I didn't mean *that* kinda payday, fool."

"What did you mean?"

"You'll find out. Caleb, you're a caution."

* * *

A large, authoritative man with stripes on his arms took them in hand. "Boys, I am Sergeant Trammell. I am going to be your father and mother from now on. Oh, you will still have officers that will give you orders, but they will mostly do it through me. If you have any problems, come to me with them. I am going to show you boys how to be soldiers."

And he began to. He showed them how to put up their larger tents, how and where to dig slit trenches

("You don't jist shit wherever the notion strikes you, fer everbody to go steppin' in and to smell up the camp"), how and where to build fires for cooking, what the various bugle calls and drum rolls meant, how to march, how to load and fire their pieces. He was a good teacher: patient, with the ability to use language they understood. They liked and admired him immensely.

Their corporal was Bill Hamman, who seemed older and better educated than most of them. He was humble, but when pressed admitted he had attended the University of Virginia, and had been a captain in the Virginia militia before moving to Texas. "At first I thought leaving the union was a bad idea, but the election of Lincoln left us no choice."

Caleb's tent mates were Bill, John, Henry, Tolly, and Pat. Their days were spent in drilling, cooking, cleaning the mud off their gear, and more drilling. After a few weeks of this routine, orders were received incorporating their company into a new regiment. The regimental commander was Colonel Hood, who addressed them thusly: "Boys, I am John Bell Hood, and I am honored to be your commanding officer. Although I was born in Kentucky, I served in Texas with the old army and consider myself a Texan like you. When this war is over and we have established our independence, I will make Texas my home.

"I know from my time in Texas that Texas boys are raised up to be obedient, God-fearing good citizens. To respect their elders and their womenfolk. To work hard. To do their duty. As soldiers here in Virginia, the eyes of others will be watching us. Watching to see if we are good people or bad people. I know that not one of you boys would ever want to do anything that would bring shame or disgrace upon yourselves or your families or Texas. When you are away from camp, be mindful of this. Show respect for the womenfolk, the old people. Make Texas, make me and your other officers proud of you.

"Another way that I know you boys are going to make Texas proud of you is when we go into action. Texans are brave. Texans do not waver in their devotion. Texans move ahead. Texans chastise the enemy. Texans smite the foe. Texans capture the enemy, or kill him. Texans capture the enemy's battle flags and proudly exhibit them after the battle. Texans are invincible!"

The regiment let out a high-pitched Rebel yell that sent chills all over Caleb and caused the hair on his neck to stand up.

"Boys," Hood continued, "soon we march north, to join with other Texas regiments in setting up a defense line between us and the Yankees. We have been honored with this important responsibility of standing between Richmond and the enemy. I am certain that you will uphold that honor, and that your actions will reflect credit upon your parents and Texas."

Again the cheers were deafening. Hood raised his hat in acknowledgement.

Chapter 5

▼

The Dallas **Spectator:** September 4, 1861

The top military leaders of our nation are, in order of rank: Samuel Cooper, Adjutant and Inspector General of the Army; Albert Sidney Johnston of Texas, hero of San Jacinto and general commanding all Confederate forces in the West; Robert E. Lee, who is well-known to Texans from many years of service in our midst; Joseph E. Johnston; and Pierre G. T. Beauregard, the latter two the victors at Manassas. With such capable men at the head of our armies, how can we not be victorious?

*   *   *

The new camp was called Camp Wigfall, for the general who commanded its brigade. It housed three regiments of Texans and one of Georgians.

The drilling continued and was expanded to include exercises involving the entire brigade. A great amount of time was devoted to constructing forts and earthworks against an expected Federal assault from the north. They sharpened the ends of logs and stuck them into the earthworks, pointing them toward the enemy lines. "Sarge, what is them things called?" Caleb asked.

"Them's called abatis."

Bill exclaimed, "I didn't join the army to be no Goddamn ditch-digger. Hell, I could of stayed home and did this shit fer my Daddy."

"Bill, the Lord is listening when you blaspheme His name this way," John declared gently.

"Are you a preacher or what? You say yer last name is what?"

"It's Martin."

"Bullshit. I think it must be Baptist. I'm gonna call you John the Baptist."

"I'll take that as a grand compliment, Bill, but I think you mean it as another blasphemy."

They all took it up; from then on he was John the Baptist.

*   *   *

A bunch of them were sitting or squatting around the fire, trying to keep warm, staring into the flames as man has done since time immemorial.

"Sergeant Trammell, how long has you been in the army?"

"Well, this one, not long. But I was in the old army, oh, about ten year."

"Where did you serve?"

"Why, I was in Texas, where you boys is from. I was in the Second Cavalry. We fit Indians, Comanch mostly. Fact a the matter, a bunch a our officers was in there with me. Bobby Lee. Sidney Johnston, he's a full general now, commanding everthing west a the mountains. Good officer. Bobby Lee was a damn good officer. Yessir, everbody liked Marse Robert. Even then you could tell he was sumpin' special. George Thomas; we called him 'Slow Trot' 'cause he had somethin' wrong with his back and he couldn't ride fast. He stayed with the Union although he is a Virginian, which I cain't unnerstand, but again they's a lotta things Ol' Sarge don't unnerstand. Why, Colonel Hood was in that outfit. Got to be a hero in a Indian fight. Got shot, by a arrow. Good officer. He was a lieutenant then."

"Was you a sergeant then?"

"Naw, I was jist a private. Didn't make sergeant 'til jist before you boys got here."

"Was General Wigfall a officer there?"

"Wigfall? Hell, no. He's a damn politician. He ain't no soldier." He spat into the fire. "He wouldn't make a boil on a good soldier's ass. He don't know no more 'bout soldierin' than I do 'bout bein' king a China." He laughed bitterly. "If it warn't fer yer *real* soldiers like Hood, Wigfall would be in a peck a trouble. And we ain't had no fightin' atall yet. Why, I have bad dreams when I think what is goin' to happen when we have a battle with *Wigfall* in charge."

"Speakin' a battle, Sarge, what is it like?"

He considered this for a while. "What you want to know is, how will you do? You boys will do fine. Sure, you'll be skeered. You show me a man fixin' to go into combat that ain't skeered, I'll show you a damn fool. You wonder if'n you'll run away; you won't. You know why you won't? Because I'll be watchin' you. And so will yer officers. And so will yer mates. You won't do nothin' to embarrass yerselves before them. And besides, you'll be too busy to think about anything, *includin'* lightin' out. You'll be doin' yer job."

He held them in thrall in this fashion for half the night.

Later Caleb asked Bill, "Do you think you'll be skeered when we go into our first fight?"

"Does a bear shit in the woods? Course I'll be skeered, fool. Didn't you hear what the Sarge said?"

"I jist hope I don't light out."

"You light out and I'll pass you like you was tied to a hitchin' post."

"Maybe neither one of us will, Bill. It jist seems to me like it'll be awful skeery, bein' shot at and all."

*   *   *

Oct. 15, 1861

Dear Liz,

I am reel sorry that I have not wrote you sooner, but they have kept us awfull buzy. What we are doing is to bild a bunch of forts and ditches and artilry embrazurs here close to the Potomic river in case the Yankees decides to try to attact us. And when we are not doing all this digging and bilding we are drilling and marching a terrible lot. It is not easy being a soljer!

Right on the other hand we have not saw no fighting. We can hear the Yankees right acrost the river and can even see them somtimes and have herd there bands playing but no shots has been fired to speak of.

Our company has it's own band, and the feller that runs it is call Gus Bailey, he has wrote a song call "The

Old Gray Mare". His wife Molly is a nurse and some say a spy, I know she passes thru the lines sometimes, oncet I seen her but didn't know her because she was got up to look so old.

There is a little town clost by call Dumfries, but we don't have time to go their much. Our camp is call Camp Wigfall for Gen. Wigfall. You may of herd of him for he was a senator. What he does mostly is drink a lot and when he has been drinking he gits all excited and thinks the Yankees is coming to attact us, so we do not git a lot of sleep somtimes. Onetime he sounded the alarm for us to fall out but our col. Hood said for us just to not pay no mind because it was just another hoo rah by Gen. Wigfall.

I like Col Hood a lot. He is very young and tall and handsum and has the sadest eyes I ever did see. He has always been a soljer and was in Texas fighting Indians before the war.

Captain Sutphin got pretty sick soon after we got to Virginia and went home. In fact a awfull lot of our people has got sick with the fever and one thing and another. I had a little spot of fever but am fine now.

I have made sevral frends. One is Bill Tardy he is a very funy boy from Mesquite. He has a lot of funy sayings which I can not write to you. He is my age except taller and is trying to grow a mustash. We rag him about his mustash being tardy like his last name.

Another frend is Tolly Johnson from around Dallas. He is 22 and is married and joined up to fight anyways. He spends a awfull lot of time writting to his wife and she writes him.

Another frend is John Martin who is reel religious and is all the time talking about God and tries to git the boys not to talk so ruff, so Bill has started to call him John the Babtist and it is starting to catch on with the rest.

Another frend is Henry Dowd who lives outside of Denton. He is reel frenlie and nice and is always lending me things or offering to lend me things and help me with my cooking or cleening the mud off my geer or picking the cooties out of my blankit and stuff such as that.

Pat McKee is a real big feller and he is reel good-natured but he is a little clumsy and has a hard time getting some of the drills and the mannuel of arms strait.

Bert Sammons is in my company but he is sevral tints down. I gess you know Ben got kilt on the way heer. He fell off the train and got runned over.

Oh I forgot to tell you that our new capt. Is name Sealy. He took over from Capt Sutphin, he seems fine but a little bit like he is not sure what to do or say. I don't think he likes me to much. We have a Sgt name of Trammel who is a old sgt from the old army and he is realy fine. He is big and tall and loud (Bill says he could go bear hunting with a switch) and he keeps us in line but also he takes care of us all the time about food and blankits and the like. He knows pretty well what we are suppose to do even if Capt Sealy don't always. There is a reel young captain in the next company name of Gaston, I wish he was ours.

I have wrote a few leters home for some of the boys who cant read or write. I would say that probly half of them cant read or write.

Well Liz I gess that is all for now. You keep on writting to me because I sure do injoy heering from you. Tell your folks hello for me and also my folks if you should see them. My folks don't read and write to good except for Jamie and I imagin hes to buzy.

Love,
Caleb

*   *   *

They were given a day off, to do as they pleased. Bill and Tolly went into Richmond. Henry said to the rest, "Would you boys like to go grabblin'?"

"What is grabblin'?" Pat inquired.

"You ain't never been grabblin'? Come on, I'll show you."

So Henry, Pat, Caleb, and John the Baptist went to the creek.

"Grabblin' is fishin' with yer hands," Henry explained. He eased into the water and began to feel under the ledges. Sure enough, in a few minutes he produced a fish.

"Hey, that's a good trick," Pat cried. "Show me how to do that." He too slipped into the water. "Say, this is real cold!"

"Means there won't be no snakes," Henry mentioned. "Too cold. You other boys come on in and I'll show all of you at oncet."

So John the Baptist and Caleb reluctantly entered the chilly water.

Henry took charge. "Come on over to this here bank. See this ledge? Jist take and feel along real slow and easy like and maybe you'll find you a fish."

John the Baptist and Pat complied. Caleb looked a bit hesitant. Henry said, "Caleb, why don't me and you try down there a ways while these two gives this place a goin' over." They waded downstream in the chest-deep water for 30 feet, where the water became much warmer because of a warm-water spring. "See, all you do is reach under the bank and jist feel along real easy until you find somethin'. Here, let me have yer hand." He took Caleb's hand, but instead of guiding it along the bank he placed it on his crotch. He was hard.

Caleb snatched his hand back. He stared at Henry in disbelief. He opened his mouth and started to say something, but instead he just turned and made his way back to the others as rapidly as he could. "I'm gittin' out. It's too cold fer me."

"Hey, Caleb, what's yer rush?" Pat yelled.

"I'm gonna git on back to camp and git into some dry clothes."

The next day Henry asked and received permission from the Sergeant to change tents. He was replaced by Eli Davis, a skinny man of 30 who always had a stick or straw in his mouth, who had just arrived from Texas. Henry had left so quickly that he had not done a thorough job of clearing out the area that Eli now occupied. Eli brought a piece of paper to Caleb. "This has got yer name on it." Caleb studied the paper: It showed a knife dripping a liquid, and above the knife was the name "Caleb".

*   *   *

"Tolly, what did you and Bill do in Richmond?"

Tolly chuckled. "We went to a whorehouse. I didn't do nothin', hadn't planned to. Bill wanted to see if he could git him some. But I knew he didn't have no money to amount to nothin'. So he was talkin' to this whore, and he says, 'How much do you charge?' and she says, 'I don't charge, I jist take cash.' So Bill says, 'You know what I mean; how much do you git?' And she says, 'I git all I can.' And then Bill, he is startin' to git all red in the face, he says, 'Goddamn it woman, I didn't come here to be made sport of, how much money do you want to give me a little?' And she says, 'A dollar.' So Bill reaches in his pocket and pulls out all his money and all he is got is four bits. So he asts me if I got any and I says you know I ain't got a nail. So he asts this whore, 'How much would you charge ol' Bill fer a *slow* hand job.' And she says, 'Don't you know it says in the Bible that it's a sin to cast yer seed upon the ground?' And Bill says, 'Hell, Madam, I'm not tryin' to live at the foot of the cross'."

They roared, except for John the Baptist.

Chapter 6

The Dallas **Spectator** September 15, 1861

Justice! At last!

The abominable General Nathaniel Lyon met his just desserts near Springfield, Missouri, when his forces were decisively defeated by Confederate troops under Sterling Price, former governor of Missouri, and Ben McCulloch, famed Texas soldier and Ranger. Lyon was killed in the battle, his body later conveyed to the Union lines by chivalrous Southerners. Prominent in the victory were the Third Texas Cavalry, recruited in Dallas a few weeks ago, under Col. Greer, the first Texans to serve outside our state. Now Missouri is open to liberation by the Confederacy.

* * *

Dec. 25, 1861
Dear Liz,

Well here it is Christmas day, the first I have ever spent away from home. I sure do miss not being abel to see you and your folks, and my Momma & Poppa &

Jamie & Annie & David. Momma allways cooks so much good food on Christmas such as ham and chicken and sweet potatos and green beens and usally a pie or two. I beter quit reminding myself of all that good food because it is starting to make my mouth water. Maybe this will be the only Christmas that I will have to be away from you all. Maybe the war will end before next Christmas.

We still have not saw no fighting. That part is good because no body has been hurt. But we lost one of the boys in my tint. You may recall I mentioned to you about a Pat McKee, well he drownded in a creek the other day. He had gone grabbling by hisself which means fishing with just your hands and I suppose he shouldn't of gone off just by hisself because they found him ded a few hours later. We don't have no idee what or how it happened. It just seems like such a shame and a tragiddy that here he come up all this way to fight Yankees and instead he drownded without never firing no shot at them. We felt awfull about it. His place has been took by Wash Benton.

It has been prety cold hear. I gess being right on the river has made it colder. We have had some snow already. That and the rain has made the camp awfull muddy. I thought I knew about mud from the farm but with so many men around you have not ever saw mud like we have.

This morning some of the ladies from Dumfries come out to our camp and brougt some food which was very wellcome. I don't know what they thought about the mud. Also it don't exactly smell like a garden out here.

Also speaking of ladies. The mother of one of our company men name of Young made us a flag, our old one was pretty beet up. She has wrote pomes like you has Liz but hers has been printed in some books and papers. Some of us calls her the Confederate Lady or The Soljers Frend.

Well Liz I will close for now. I hope you have had a nice Christmas. Please give my best regards to your family and also if you happen to see my family also give them my best wishes. I am doing fine hear and am not worried.

Love,
Caleb

P.S. The river is froze over and the Yankees is just on the other side. The other day some of us went out on the ice and some Yankee boys was also out on the ice. They was dressed so funy you would never beleve it. They had on red shirts instead of blue and these here reel baggy pants. We ast them if they was from Turkey or what and they says no they is from New York. They are called zoo-ahs or zoo-vahs or some such crazy like name. They also said they was going to whup us good and propper first battle we is in against them. We just laughed and throwed ice at them but they was to far away to be hitted. Also they made sport of how we talk with words like reckon and yonder so then we rilly pored it on thick.

*   *   *

"Boys, I need six volunteers fer a kinda dangerous job," Sergeant Trammell bellowed.

John the Baptist said, "I'll do 'er." Caleb indicated he would go, as did Wash and Eli. Tolly and Bill hung back.

"Who's leadin' the job?" demanded Bill.

"I am," replied the Sergeant.

"Then I'll go," said Bill. "If it was gonna be Captain Sealy or some other officer that don't know shit from macaroni, huh-uh. But I'll foller you, Sarge."

"Thankee, Bill. You wanta make it six, Tolly?"

Tolly was not enthusiastic. But the peer pressure was decisive. "I guess so."

They were joined by three other men from a nearby tent. "What we gonna do is some scoutin' up towards the Yankee lines. Check on their movements and dispositions. Bring yer pieces and twenny rounds and yer canteens, but no packs. We will leave at two in the mornin'."

*   *   *

The patrol walked past their own pickets into a hushed night. They stayed in single file, walking down the country road silently, their white breath stabbing the darkness. Ground fog hovered over the area like levitating cotton, giving it a ghostly and unworldly look.

After a three mile walk they came to a two-story frame house. The Sergeant gathered his men tightly around him and whispered, "We need to find out if'n anybody's in there. Could be Yankee soldiers." But as they tried the door it was open, and a look inside revealed no furniture. "Abandoned, I'd allow. S'pose they couldn't decide which side they was on. You boys kin set down and take a pull from yer canteens, but no smokin'. We'll go ahead on in a few minutes."

Suddenly outside they heard the sound of horses. A shouted command to halt and dismount made the picture clear: Yankees!

The Sergeant was galvanized. "Pick up yer pieces, boys, and you two cover the front door! Caleb, Bill, watch the back door! Tolly, take that window, Eli, the other one! The rest of you, upstairs! If you hear firin', you open up on them from up there! Hurry!"

As one of the Union soldiers walked onto the front porch he was shot in the chest. The remainder of the Northern patrol recoiled a few yards and fired their carbines at the house. "Surround the house! Pour it on them Rebs!"

Several of the bluecoats were soon hit. A horse was observed riding hard for the Northern lines. "He's a-going fer help," said the Sergeant. "We've got to git outa here quick or we're all dead or captured. 'Pears like they's too many of 'em fer us to shoot our way through. I'm gonna try somethin'." He went upstairs and, in his loudest voice shouted, "We're saved, boys, I kin see Hampton's Legion a-comin' this way fast, must be a hunderd of 'em!"

Incredibly the ruse worked. Within three minutes the bluecoats were in their saddles and high-tailing it north, leaving their casualties behind. A Rebel yell issued from many throats. Then Sergeant Trammell announced, "That's enough celebratin', boys. We best ske-daddle, fer that feller that rode fer help jist might bring a passel a Yankees right back, so we won't stretch our luck. Line up outside."

But only eight besides the Sergeant lined up. "Who's missin'?" They rushed back inside for a hurried search.

Upstairs, collapsed near a remote window, was Wash. He had a hole in his forehead just above the right eye, not a big hole at all, and he was quite dead. They carried him downstairs and devised a litter from some of their shirts, and alternated carrying him back to camp. "We ain't givin' them Yankees the satisfaction a knowin' they kilt one a our boys."

The brigade was proud of the great joke it played on the Yankees, but saddened at their very first battle death.

*   *   *

Later in their tent Eli, stick in his mouth, said, "Pore ol' Wash, seems like he jist got here, and he went and got hisself kilt."

"It was the Lord's will," proclaimed John the Baptist.

"Talk about luck. Sarge jist called out some names to stay downstairs and ordered everbody else upstairs," Caleb noted. "It coulda jist as easy been me or any one a you boys standin' at that window 'stead a Wash."

Tolly was thoughtful. "You know, in a way it may have been a blessin' that Wash was kilt. Bein' shot in the head and all. If he'd lived he mighta been blind. I cain't think of anything worse than bein' blind."

"Or even worser, it might have did damage to his brain so's he'd never be right in his head agin," said Eli. "Head wounds is the thing I fear most. Wouldn't want to spend the rest a my life bein' blind *ner* crazy."

Caleb said, "I think a belly wound would be worser to me. Maybe have yer guts a-hangin' out." He shuddered. "What about you, Bill? What kinda wound would be the worst to you?"

Bill reflected for a half minute. "Wouldn't wanna git shot in the crown jewels," he said, indicating his crotch. They all nodded in grim agreement.

"Well, I guess we done been in our first battle," offered Caleb.

"I wouldn't call that no *battle*, more like jist a fight or a skirmish. I think of a battle as bein' outside with lots more men," Bill observed.

"Was you boys skeered?" asked Tolly.

'I wadn't too skeered," Caleb said. "Guess I was too busy to be skeered. What supprised me was the noise. Them muskets sure does make a lot a racket, don't they?"

"Yeah, inside like that," Eli pointed out. "And the smoke. If we'da did much more firin' I couldn't of saw nothin' atall."

Bill added, "I felt purty easy havin' the Sarge there. I thought he done real good."

"He's been in fights before, with Indians," said John the Baptist.

"So we *still* don't know how we'll do in a real battle, does we?" Bill's look was one of self-important wisdom.

*   *   *

After everyone was supposedly asleep and Caleb was still awake, reliving the fight, he heard one of the men masturbating.

*   *   *

Dec. 25, 1861
My dearest Caleb,

Well here it is Christmas day and you are not here. I am happy that my folks is here but how much better if only you could be with me and we could talk and laugh and go walking and hold hands and kiss one another. But that is not possible so I will try to be strong. I don't want to make you sad by writing sad things but I do want you to know how much I miss my sweet Caleb. I miss you all the time, ever day but it just seems more deep at Christmas.

I surely hope you are safe and warm and getting plinty to eat.

My days has been busy. Me and Paw works pretty near ever day doing the chores and putting things right. I have to be like a man because they are no brothers to help Paw but I am use to it. I never have minded working as you know. And I know Paw appreciates it even if he don't tell me about it a lot.

I went to church Sunday and everbody asked about you as usual. We have had a mild winter so far and have not lost no stock yet.

Paw says we been lucky the Comanches have not come after us but he wonders how much longer that luck will hold out.

I saw Quince the other day and he said to give you his best. He is really having to work harder with the 2 Sammons boys gone and 1 of them dead but he is not complaining. I do think he has lost some wate.

Caleb when I lay on my bed ever night I think about you and pray that you are all right. One of these days

soon we will be together and I will be the happyest girl in Texas.
   Love forever,
   Liz

Chapter 7

The Dallas **Spectator,** January 1, 1862

The New Year promises success for our national experiment. Federals have been swept from Texas, and millions of dollars in military equipment seized thereby. Oklahoma is occupied by our forces. Our brave men are defending Southern territory from Richmond to Missouri. May our patriotic fervor burn bright and hot, and sustain our independence, and bring this war to a quick conclusion, so that by Christmas 1862 all our brave men will be back to home and hearth and loved ones.

*   *   *

Jan. 20, 1862
Dear Liz,

Well its reel cold hear, I sure hope it is not this cold in Tex. Thank God we are not still in tints, we have bilt us a caben or a hut out of planks, at lest on 3 sides, it is a lot like a log caben and it is a lot warmer than a tint I garuntee. We keep a fire going on the south side where there aint no complet wall. We do have a few rats I gess they are trying to stay warm just like we are. But at lest the flies & skeeters is gone for now. And the mud is froze.

I ast the sarge how come they don't just let us go home in the winter when there is no fighting anyhow and that way they wouldn't have to feed us and he says lots of the boys wouldn't come back in the spring.

It is to cold to drill and so we are not reel buzy. We even git to lay up in bed some days until 7 when they fall us out for role call and sick call. Then we cook somthing to eat usally bacon and we eat a lot of biskits and corn-bread and beef but the beef is not the best not like a fresh kilt cow at home its more like reel old or like its been in a can and we don't care much for it none of us.

I don't know if I told you that I was in a house a while back that had been in the middle of a batlefield and it had a cannonball stuk in the wall.

There are lots of games to play like foot races & kick ball and town ball with 2 bases and rassling and even some of the boys boxs but not me because I don't like to git hit on my nose. When it is to cold to git out and do those games we stay in doors and play card games like poker or 21 or a game call keno or a game call you-ker or some such as that. We are more likely to play these close to pay day also chuck-a-luck which is a dice game. Some of the boys drinks even in the day time speshully close to pay day but you know I don't much care for the taste of it Liz.

We also do a lot of hunting like for posums and rabbits and all kinds of birds up hear in Va., infact Liz I found me a little criple rabit one day with a hurt leg that couldn't hop away and so I have bilt a little cage for him and I call him Danny and all the boys likes him and feeds him so much I feer he will git so fat that we want be abel to see his eyes. He is a frenlie little feller and I think he knows me.

Speaking of animals a pole-cat got in one of the cabins the other day I gess he was cold and he sprayed the boys in their reel good and propper and they had to burn the tint and about all there close and none of the other boys would git near them and we been ragging them every sense.

Sevral of the boys has fidels and banjos and so we never lack for music & some of the boys will dance and cut up when they are playing and it is a caushon to watch. Also the camp has sevral bands and they play ever so offen and we get to heer them. My favrits is Home Sweet Home and Lissen to the Monkinbird & the Bony Blu Flag and Just Before the Batle Mother, and Goober Pees and Lorena. Matter of fack sometimes when the wind is right we can heer the Yankee bands playing and they do some of the same songs speshuly Home Sweet Home. And of corse when they is playing ours or sometimes even theres we will sing along with the band. I ast Bill who don't sing much if he can carry a toon and he says I can *carry* a toon but the trubble comes when I have to *unload* it. I rember your sweet voice from when you used to sing at church and also at school. And I also rember the dances we went to togather, and how good you always smelled when you and me danced with one another.

Something reel funy happened the other day, a suttler come out to camp with his wagon load of truck like candie & smokes and oisters and such and he has his prices awfull high because he knows we caint always git into town to by things so he is not to popler, so what we done is while some of the boys talked to him at the frunt some of us took a lot of his stuff from the back & then when he come to see about what was a going on at the back the boys in the frunt got there pokets full. Well he got all mad & hollerin but we lit out befor he could do anything. We all et candie for sevral days. Some of the boys et oisters but they look to funy to me.

Well Liz I have run on about long enuf, you keep on with your sweet leters as I truly injoy heering from you. My best to your folks.

Love,
Caleb

   *   *   *

Captain Sealy was not happy. His face was red and his eyes bulged as he addressed the assembled company.

"I am ashamed of you men! I keep getting reports of stealing from the farmers hereabouts. Chickens. Pigs. Pies cooling on window ledges. Even fence posts, for Christ's sake! Is nothing sacred to you men? How were you raised? Don't you realize that these people are on the same side we are? And then yesterday some of you men nearly cleaned out a sutler. I tell you I won't have my men stealing! We're going to put a stop to all this activity or I'll know the reason why! Dismiss them, Sergeant!"

Back in their tent, they guffawed. "I thought I was gonna have to put my shirt-tail in my mouth so I wouldn't laugh in his face out there," Bill chuckled.

"If'n they'd feed us better and give us enough wood to keep warm we wouldn't have to go makin' them midnight requisitions," Tolly added.

"Amen to that!" cried Eli.

John the Baptist demurred. "The captain's right, you know. Stealin' is a sin. You boys are flirting with the lake a fire when you take what belongs to other folks."

"Come on, John the Baptist. That sutler deserved to be cleaned out," said Caleb. "He charges us three or four prices for all that truck he sells. *He's* the one is stealin'."

Eli said, "Why, that pig I come in with the other day, I kilt in self-defense. He was a-chargin' me with blood in his eye, and it were him or me. You boys wouldn't want to have that pig in here a-livin' with you, now would you?"

"Might be a improvement over you, matter a fack," Bill said, causing everyone to laugh, even John the Baptist and Eli.

Captain Sealy was in the hut, and they snapped to attention. "Well, I can see that my little talk had no effect whatever on you hooligans. Walker! Get that smile off your face! I'll get your attention one way or the other. Mr. Walker, you will stand sentry duty all night, over the privy. Is that understood?"

"Yessir."

"Report to that post immediately!" He left them.

"Goddamn, Caleb, I don't know why he's a-pickin' on you," said a sympathetic Bill.

"I don't neither, 'cept he's been a-lookin' at me kinda funny fer weeks now. Well, I guess I better git my longees on and git out there."

*   *   *

It was one of those clear nights when seemingly millions of stars were visible. And whereas on a summer night the air was alive with the sounds of crickets and bullfrogs, on this frigid winter night there were no sounds of life save the occasional ones made by the army: snoring, walking, challenges by sentries. Caleb kept warm by stamping his feet. Fortunately the wind was light.

During the long night he thought often of his Secret. None of the other boys seemed to have any difficulty with it; at least he had not heard them speak of it. Was he the only one in the brigade who had it? If he was, he hoped that it would not come out. He liked all of them real well, and hated to think that his Secret would alienate them, maybe even cause a loss of morale.

More than once he comforted himself by recalling Liz's poem, which he had long since memorized.

> Caleb, O my dear Caleb!
> Must you go off to war?
> These places they are sending you
> They seem so very far.
> Sweetheart you know I love you,
> That my heart will always be true.
> Because you are so very brave
> This thing you had to do.
> When you see the stars come out at night
> Oh please remember me.
> The many dreams and plans we made
> Down under the old oak tree.
> I will go there often
> Pretending you are there.

Some wild flowers I will gather
And place one in my hair.
When this war is over
I know you'll return to me.
We will be reunited
Down under the old oak tree.

An occasional soldier would come to use the privy; if they recognized him they might speak or nod in their half-awake state. Mostly they ignored him and a few even snickered at his plight.

Then Henry came. Caleb was nervous about how to regard him, as they had not been face-to-face since the creek incident. "How you been, Henry? I ain't saw you in weeks, leastways not to speak to."

Henry was sullen. He looked around furtively before replying. "How many boys has you tole about me?"

Caleb was surprised. "Why, I ain't tole nobody. Didn't figger it was nobody's binness."

"I don't believe you, Caleb Walker. Some a the boys has been lookin' at me funny. 'Specially Bill Tardy."

Caleb was distracted by that expression Henry had just used. What was it he had said? Oh, yes, "lookin' at me funny". It was an expression he himself had used just a few hours before in regard to Captain Sealy. Suppose the captain had been looking at him funny because he thought that Caleb shared Henry's peculiarity? But Caleb was not allowed the luxury of continued rumination on this line of thought, for Henry was persisting in his inquisition.

"You tole Bill Tardy, didn't you?"

"I tole you, Henry, I ain't tole nobody." He smelled liquor on Henry's breath.

"Then how come he's been a-lookin' at me so peculiar, grinnin' kinda silly, like he thinks he knows somethin'?"

"Well, come to think of it, way back in Texas when we was a-marchin' towards Houston, Bill used to say things to me 'bout you."

"Like what?"

"Oh, somethin' about how you was like my shadow and that there would come a pay day about you some kinda way."

Henry waxed reflective. "Bill's a damn trouble maker. One a these days somebody may jist fix Mr. Bill's wagon."

"What do you mean, Henry?"

But Henry turned and left.

* * *

Caleb was not exactly sure when his tour of duty as privy sentry was supposed to end. The captain had said all night, so he assumed that when most of the camp was up and about he was done. He went to his hut to find the boys beginning to stir. Tolly and John the Baptist were starting some bacon and coffee.

"Well, was it bad out there?" John the Baptist inquired.

"Wasn't too bad." He sat on his bed.

The captain came in. He was livid. "Walker, I thought I ordered you to stand sentry duty all night!"

"I did, sir." He was on his feet.

"No you didn't! You are in *here*, aren't you? You haven't been relieved!"

Caleb was trembling, from fatigue as well as the mortification of the dressing down he was getting. "Captain, sir, I ain't been in here more'n two or three minutes. When the camp got to stirrin' I figgered…."

"You are not supposed to figger, soldier! That's for officers and sergeants to do. When I assign you to a duty I expect you to continue to do it until I relieve you *personally*, is that clear to you, you dolt?"

"Yessir."

The captain's eyes swept the hut. "What in the hell is that thing?" He was looking at the crippled rabbit in the cage.

None of them said anything.

"Who does that thing belong to?"

Finally Caleb spoke up. "It's mine, sir. That's Danny, he's a little rabbit I found out in…"

"That figures!" thundered Captain Sealy. "This ain't no damned menagerie. I want that thing out of here, do you understand me, Walker?"

"Yessir."

The captain left in a fury.

"Talk about wakin' up on the wrong side a the bed!" exclaimed Bill.

"What is a dolt?" Eli asked.

"I don't think it's no compliment," Bill replied.

A few minutes passed in nervous, self-conscious silence. Finally Caleb said, "Well, I guess I got to let Danny go."

"If you do, somethin'll git 'im sure as the world," John the Baptist opined.

"I know! Let's hide him out in the woods somewheres he'll be safe. Then we kin go out and feed him now and agin." Tolly was pleased with his suggestion.

They found a hollow in a tree high enough off the ground so that predators could not get at the rabbit easily. Then the conspirators returned to their hut and their day.

Chapter 8

The Dallas **Spectator,** February 3, 1862

Beware the apostate! George Thomas, a Virginian who served in Texas with the Second Cavalry, and who failed to join his state when it seceded, has won a Union victory in Kentucky. May a righteous Creator smite this turncoat the way he smote Lyon in Missouri.

* * *

The new man, replacing the dead Wash, was Tom Mason, who turned out to be the best cook in the hut. Tom was heavy-set, with a pleasant look. He showed them how to cook potatoes in their jackets, corn in their shucks, and how to make cush. "What you do is, you fry all the grease outa yer bacon, then you put the bacon in a pot with water, cut up some a that bad beef, add cornbread er biscuits er both, and stew it until the water is gone." It was surprisingly good.

They were sitting around the fire one evening enjoying Tom's cush. Tolly was morose.

"What's eatin' you, Tolly? You look like you got some bad news from home," John the Baptist observed.

Tolly was hesitant in his reply. "It's my wife, Sally. She's havin' a purty hard time of it. She says how she misses me and how lonesome she gits and she's been purty sick. I jist wonder did I make a mistake by joinin' up and goin' off and leavin' her the way I done."

They all affected sympathetic looks. All except Bill. "The woman oughtn't write all that sad shit to you. Don't she rillize there ain't a damn thing you kin do, off up here in Virginia? Jist like a woman, causin' trouble."

John the Baptist disagreed. "I think she ought to write Tolly jist what she's a–feeling'. It must be awful hard on her, bein' left alone. At least Tolly's got lotsa friends around."

Eli entered in. "I go along with Bill. The woman ought to rillize that Tolly's got enough on his mind without havin' no whiney wife writin' letters that tears him up. Tolly cain't jist pick up and go back to Texas to hold her hand."

"You boys is talkin' about Tolly's troubles like he was somewheres else. The man is a-settin' right here a-havin' to lissen to y'all a-puttin' his woman down," said an exasperated Caleb. "It's a wonder he don't git up and whang somebody on the mouth."

"No," said Tolly in a mollifying tone, "that's alright, I don't mind whatever you boys has to say about it. We is all friends here."

Eli declared, "I think you're lucky, Tolly."

"What do you mean?"

"I mean I feel lucky bein' away from the one *I* left back home. This gal was like a itch you cain't scratch. No never mind how bad I treated her, or how much I ignored her, she was always a-comin' back fer more. Wanted me to marry her so bad she could taste it."

Bill sneered, "Hell, I kin unnerstand that easy. Why, as good a catch as you is, Eli, I wager ever woman and girl in the county was a-pantin' after you, stick in yer mouth an' all." A general snicker went around the group.

"Naw, I ain't a-claimin' to be the Romeo a the county."

"Romeo!" several of them mocked.

Eli continued, "This pore gal jist had the hots fer me. Wouldn't give me no peace. All I done was to poke her a few times and I reckon I musta hit some kinda nerve or somethin'. She was over at my place night and day, a'wantin' me to do it to her some more. That's why I joined up, to git away from ol' Rose."

"She musta been so ugly she would scare the buzzards offa gut wagon. You shouldn't of been such a good poker, Romeo," Bill grinned. "Anybody else here because they was doin' too good a job at servicin' the womenfolk back home? What about you, John the Baptist?"

"I ain't never been married so I ain't never been with no woman."

"Hell, boy, you don't have to be married. That's jist the password," Bill snorted. "What about you, Caleb boy? I know that little gal a yours writes pomes to you. Was you a-pokin' her back there on the farm?"

Caleb reddened. "That ain't a lot a yer binness, Bill. And she jist wrote me one pome, fer a goin'-away present."

Bill was jubilant. "I know you been a-pokin' her, 'cause if you wasn't you'da said no, but since you said it ain't none a my binness, that means you been a-doin' it."

"You think you're so damn smart, don't you?" Caleb was more miffed than any of them had ever seen him. Bill thought it the better part of wisdom to change the subject.

"Tom, we ain't heerd from you. What about the womenfolk in your life?"

Tom sniffed. "Well, there ain't much to tell. I've had me a few rolls in the hay. Enjoyed ever one of 'em. Hope to git back home soon and do it some more."

The tension subsided.

*   *   *

Tom heard tell of the pet rabbit they had hid in the woods. "Next time one a you goes out there, take me and show me."

Caleb took Tom out that evening. To their horror, the rabbit had been killed, each of its legs and its head cut off. They gave it a pathetic burial.

Next day Henry strolled by their hut. "Et any rabbit lately?" he smirked.

Caleb had to be restrained.

Bill reasoned, "If you kill that sorry son-of-a-bitch, cain't you jist hear yerself sayin' at yer court-martial, 'I done it because he kilt my rabbit'?"

"That's right," added Tom. "Unless you git lucky enough to git a court full a rabbit lovers."

Caleb let it go, for the time being.

Chapter 9

The Dallas **Spectator,** March 3, 1862

Another disaster! Forts Henry and Donelson have been lost, apparently through either cowardice or ineptitude. It seems that the commander, General Floyd, decided the fort should be surrendered but he didn't want to be taken prisoner, so he turned command over to General Pillow who in turn abdicated responsibility to the unfortunate General Buckner. If there is any good news in this catastrophe it is that the cavalry Commander, Colonel Forrest, refused to surrender his men and led them out to fight another day. We need more men like Forrest.

*   *   *

It was time to leave their winter quarters. They had a new brigade commander, Wigfall having resigned to enter the Confederate Senate. Sergeant Trammell was ecstatic. "Hood is our new commander. And he's a general now."

"Who has took his place over us?"

"Marshall. I don't know how he'll do. He's another damn politician like Wigfall. And maybe worser than that, he's a newspaper man. Only good thing I know about him is he don't like that fool Sam Houston."

"Why don't you like ol' Sam, Sarge?"

"Because he tried to keep Texas in the Union!"

They packed their personal belongings and marched south to the vicinity of a picturesque town located beside a broad river, with hills and ridges behind the town.

"What's the name a that town, Sarge?"

"Fredericksburg."

"And what's that river called?"

"You boys sure is full a questions today. It's the Rappahannock."

"Oh, yeah, that's the one that George Washington is s'posed to have threw a dollar acrost," cried an excited Caleb.

"Where'd you hear that?" John the Baptist wanted to know.

"Miz Stallcup taught us that in school."

"Seems like a damn fool thing to me, throwin' money away," Bill observed.

They put up their tents. It was still very cold. "Sarge, does we have time to build us some more huts here?"

"Naw, I don't think so. The word is we ain't gonna be here too long a time."

They settled in and cooked rations. Tom, by inclination on his part and default by the others, had become the chief cook. He decried the dearth of coffee, but furnished his own solution: boiling dried corn, which they had in plenitude. "It ain't coffee, but it's hot."

"How come you knows so much about cookin', Tom?"

He tried to look modest. "Oh, I picked up a few idees from my Maw and Paw, and then when I was with the Texas Rangers…"

"The Texas Rangers! You ain't never mentioned nothin' 'bout bein' in no Texas Rangers afore," cried Eli.

"Now don't go makin' nothin' big about it. All I was was I was a cook fer 'em. Done it fer, oh, little over a year."

"What was y'all up to?" Eli wanted to know.

"Mostly chasin' Comanches, down around Austin and San Antone."

"Was you ever in any fightin'?" Caleb asked.

"Oncet I was. We was camped out on this crick and some a them Comanch killed our outposts and was in our camp cuttin' throats afore we knowed it, and I was jist lucky enough to wake up with this Injun a-sneakin' towards me with the biggest knife you ever seen, studyin' about takin' my scalp, and I shot the sucker right in the mouth. Scared the mule shit outa me."

"Damn, that's excitin'," exclaimed Tolly.

"A little more excitin' than I had bargained fer as a cook. I quit that mornin'. Figgered, big as I am, I made too big a target fer them redskins."

First thing next morning Sergeant Trammell was calling for volunteers. John the Baptist, Eli, Bill, Tom and Caleb all indicated they would go, but Tolly declined. "I think I'll sit out this dance."

There turned out to be nearly fifty of them. Their assignment was to go back to the just-abandoned old camp and destroy it. All they carried were their pieces with twenty rounds, canteens, and some of them had extra powder. The trek back to the old camp was uneventful, slowed by the mud churned up by the withdrawn brigade and its baggage wagons and ambulances. Caleb had a chance to compare farms in Virginia with those in Texas. The Virginia farms were generally smaller but had a more prosperous look. The outbuildings were built better, for one thing, and there was more water, more trees, more livestock. And the farmhouses tended to look more substantial.

The camp was mostly intact but littered. Their approach had been silent. In the headquarters cabin, sifting through the trash left by General Hood's staff, were four Yankee soldiers, who could not have been more surprised to look up and see a grinning brace of Rebel soldiers pointing muskets at them. Bill ordered, "Don't even wiggle. I don't think you boys wants to give us a excuse to shoot y'all. Caleb, take their guns away from 'em."

Sergeant Trammell was delighted with this unexpected bonus. "You two boys done good. Keep a close eye on 'em while we finish distroyin' this place."

They set to work firing the huts, using some of the powder. Rats began to run everywhere. A few of the men took shots at them until the sergeant put a stop to it.

"You want a bunch a Yankees a-comin' in to see what's the ruckus all about?"

Their work done, the old camp in flames, the detail started back towards Fredericksburg and the new camp. The captured Yankees were disconsolate. Caleb actually found himself feeling a little sorry for these boys. He tried to make light conversation. "Where is you boys from?"

"Wisconsin," was the barely audible reply.

"That's a awful long ways from here, ain't it?" They said nothing. "We is from Texas." Still no answer, or even a hint that they had heard what Caleb was saying. He began to study them. Immediately he envied them their uniforms, especially their hats and boots, which were such extravagant contrasts to his shabby counterparts. One of them, the corporal, was older, perhaps thirty, and wore by far the most disgusted look of the group. The other three wore no insignia of rank and were about Caleb's own age. Their demeanor was more that of naughty boys caught smoking behind the smokehouse.

They got back to camp well after dark. Tolly had prepared supper and listened eagerly to their saga. "Maybe I ought to of went with y'all. But I sure did need to write Sal a letter. I ain't wrote her in a week."

Caleb reflected that he felt pretty good if he wrote Liz once a month. But he said nothing.

*   *   *

The sergeant had been right: they were not to remain here for long. General Hood addressed the entire brigade:

"Men, it appears that the enemy is not going to make an attack on Richmond in this area, but instead is going to advance from the east, up the peninsula formed by the York and James Rivers. Therefore we have been ordered to depart this place and go put ourselves between the enemy and our capital. The long-awaited battle is imminent. Will you men of Texas acquit yourselves well?"

His answer was a terrifying Rebel yell.

They walked out of their camp in a driving rain which soon turned to sleet and then snow. The men walked with heads bowed, each man watching the feet of the soldier in front of him so as to avoid confronting the precipitation that inhibited his vision. "So this is the sunny south," said Tom.

"That's right, you missed the shank a the winter with us," observed Eli. "Hell, this is a *purty* day compared with some we had."

"Then I'm glad I missed 'em."

Their progress was terribly slow, the mud seemingly deeper with every step. Frequently men had to put shoulders to the supply wagons to free them from the ubiquitous muck. At night they were forced to pitch their tents on wet ground, and firewood that could be ignited was scarce, causing them to resort to tearing down fences, even outhouses and sheds to supply their cooking fires. These filchings, coupled with the inevitable stealing of pigs and chickens, did not endear them to the Virginia farmers.

After a dozen miserable days they reached a railroad which transported them to their destination: Yorktown.

"I learned in school that this is where the Revolutionary War ended. This is the place where the British surrendered to General Washington," Caleb announced to a weary, muddy, largely indifferent group.

"Wouldn't it be nice if *this* war ended here," said Tolly.

"It will if it's the Lord's will," John the Baptist pontificated.

They were ordered to entrench. "I sure am happy they are gonna let us dig into the mud," said Bill sarcastically. "I ain't saw no mud since we left Texas." This drew an appreciative laugh all around.

Soon they learned to appreciate the trenches. Federal snipers opened up a sporadic fire on them, one of the bullets knocking Tom's hat off and causing all of them to dive into the sloshy bottom of the trench.

"Now I know why we dug these ditches," breathed a shaken Tom.

"I don't know 'bout you boys, but I ain't a-gonna jist lay on my belly in this slop and let them Yankees use me fer no target practice," announced an irritated Bill. "Where is them Goddamn bullets comin' from?"

They peeked out of the trench and looked for tell-tale smoke from the Union snipers. "There's one, see in that tree over yonder on the left!" cried Tolly.

"Yeah, I see the bastard." Bill hoisted his Springfield out of the trench and took careful aim. At last he fired, and the Yankee came tumbling out of the tree. After he hit the ground he twitched for a long time.

"You got 'im, Bill!" Congratulations were forthcoming from all of them. Just as they were beginning to feel safe again, in came another round, knocking up dirt not four inches from John the Baptist.

"There's another one shootin' at us!" Again they surveyed the enemy's lines. The next smoke came from a shallow rifle pit. They all fired at the approximate area of the pit, only to be answered by another round that zinged over their heads. As fast as the six of them could load and fire they did so until they silenced the Northern sniper. "Don't know if we got 'im or he jist knocked off fer supper," Tom said.

*   *   *

They remained thus for many days, then were ordered to retreat back up the peninsula. None of them was sorry to leave those trenches.

"Boys, we are gonna be the rear guard," said Sergeant Trammell. "That means we got to pertect the main body. If we let 'em git by us, our supply wagons may be took by the bluecoats, not to mention a bunch a our boys gittin' kilt or captured. So keep a sharp eye out fer cavalry and infantry."

It was a weird sensation, looking over their shoulders. Some of them took to walking backwards, until they stumbled in the mud. Captain Sealy rode to the rear frequently. When he did, he could usually find fault with something Caleb was doing. "Walker, are you asleep?" "Walker, that's no way to carry your piece!" "Walker, keep up, Goddamnit!" "For God's sake, Walker, you're not *watching* your rear; a Yankee could walk up and stick his bayonet right up your ass and you would just look surprised." Each time after he rode away Caleb would just shake his head.

Bill said, "I don't know why he's got a cuckleburr in his ass about you, Caleb boy, but he sure do."

Chapter 10

The Dallas **Spectator,** April 17, 1862

Worse news could not be imagined! The finest officer in the Confederate armies, commander of the West, is dead. Albert Sidney Johnston has fallen in Tennessee, bravely leading a charge against the foe. Ironically, his surgeon had been sent by the general to attend a wounded Federal when Johnston was shot, and he bled to death before professional help could be summoned. His replacement is Beauregard.

Prominent among the units performing heroically in this engagement near Pittsburg Landing were Terry's Texas Rangers. We have learned that Colonel Terry was killed earlier at Woodsonville, Kentucky, which ironically is his native state, but the unit voted to keep the name in his honor.

Sidney Johnston is the second general officer from Texas to be lost in the West. At Elkhorn Tavern in Arkansas in March Ben McCulloch gave his life for the cause.

*   *   *

"Boys, we are needed." The sergeant's voice had an urgency in it.

Captain Sealy spoke to the entire company. "Yankees are landing from transports all along the river. General Hood expects that the brigade will at least halt their advance, and perhaps even be able to push them back into the river. If we don't, Richmond is in peril. Let's do our duty, men. Oh, by the way, General Hood has ordered that no one will load his piece yet. We want to wait until we get past our own pickets to load. The general wants to achieve surprise and he fears some soldier may accidentally discharge his weapon and give our advance away."

Bill said to his mates, "So we are fixin' to walk straight toward the Yankees without no bullets in our guns. I tole you these officers don't know shit from shoe polish." He surreptitiously loaded his musket.

"Bill, you oughtn't do that. You heard what the captain said," whispered a plaintive Caleb.

"To hell with the Captain."

They formed into line of battle and advanced. They had done this many times in drill but this was the first time in an actual combat situation, and hundreds of pulses quickened at the prospect of action. A few men wet their pants.

After they had walked a half mile across a pasture with the occasional tree, General Hood rode out in front of them. Caleb thought he looked magnificent on his horse: tall, erect, authoritative. They kept moving toward the river, still with no orders to load. Suddenly a Yankee corporal appeared, not 20 yards from the general. He raised his rifle and pointed it at a startled Hood. A shot rang out, but it was the Northern soldier who fell. Hood looked around. Bill was just lowering his musket.

The general said nothing to Bill. Instead he addressed the entire brigade. "Load! Fix bayonets! Advance!"

The next hours were a jumble of noise, smoke, shouted orders, falling comrades, dry throats, loading, firing, advancing. At last as they neared the river, the Federal gunboats began to shell them, and they were ordered to retire.

On his way back Caleb saw a Confederate soldier cutting the throat of a wounded Yankee. He stopped and watched in horror as the Reb then removed the dead man's shoes and knapsack, then went through his pockets. Finished with his grim work, the soldier rose and headed for his own lines. It was Henry Dowd.

* * *

Back at camp, all was confusion as the soldiers looked for their mates and chattered excitedly about their experiences. "Where is Tom? Where's Eli?"

* * *

Caleb asked Bill, "Was you skeered?"

"Didn't rilly have time to think about it. Was you?"

"Not really. What about you, John the Baptist?"

"Fear is a thing that is a waste of time. If the Lord decides to take you, He will. There ain't no use in fearin' what's gonna be."

"Was you skeered, Tolly?"

He did not answer immediately. He seemed preoccupied. Finally he replied, "What'll happen to Sal if'n I git kilt?"

* * *

The sergeant had a grim look. "Eli is in the hospital. He got hit in the arm. I don't know how bad it is."

"What about Tom?"

"He didn't make it."

"I s'pose he's fixed us a meal fer the last time," said a saddened Caleb.

Chapter 11

▼

The Dallas **Spectator,** May 11, 1862

The long-awaited Yankee assault on Richmond has begun, with McClellan's masses moving up the peninsula formed by the York and James Rivers. Among the staunch defenders of our nation's capital is Hood's Brigade, which helped repulse an attack at Eltham's Landing. We are confident Joe Johnston will prove more than a match for McClellan, with such brave Texans as Hood possesses.

*   *   *

The brigade was allowed to remain in camp for only four days to lick its wounds from its first engagement, then was set on the march again. Eli rejoined them, sans stick-in-mouth. "Damn near choked on it when I was hit." He still had a bandage on his left arm.

Just south of Richmond General Hood addressed them:

"Men, we are asked to do a little play-acting. It is known that there are Northern spies in Richmond, so we are going to fool them. As we walk through the city, make yourselves as conspicuous as possible. Let it be known that we are heading for the Shenandoah Valley. This deception will benefit our cause."

Bill cried out, "General, kin we stop in a few bars on the way through? That way we kin *really* loosen up our tongues fer them spies."

Maybe it was because Hood recognized that Bill was the one who had saved his life. "I have no objection to that, soldier. Just don't stay *too* long in the bars." He smiled and the brigade laughed, then cheered.

It took half a day for them thus to work their way through the capital. On the other side they were loaded into trains and headed westward.

"What do you s'pose this is all about?" Caleb asked.

"If you ast me, I think the whole bunch of 'em has lost their minds. Here the Yankees is by the bushel out east a here, threatenin' to take Richmond, and we're headin' west," said an indignant Bill. "I been tellin' you boys that they don't know shit from sorghum syrup. They don't know no more about runnin' a army than a hog knows about Sunday."

"At least you got to stop in town and have you a beer," Tolly pointed out.

"You wait, we'll pay fer that beer many fold," replied Bill.

"Bill, you wouldn't be happy if you was hung with a new rope," Caleb smiled.

The Shenandoah Valley was lovely: verdant, prosperous, tranquil. And they stayed there exactly one night.

The forced march back toward the east was led by "Stonewall" Jackson. Caleb thought that he was the strangest-looking man he had ever seen. "Reminds me of a Old Testament prophet."

"You know they call him 'Old Blue Light' fer the look out of his eyes," Tolly said.

"I feel safe under him," said John the Baptist. "The man is very religious, very close to God."

"The man looks crazy to me," Bill said. "Why, he dresses like a common tramp. He looks worser than we do. And why does he hold one arm up most all the time?"

As they walked toward the enemy in his thousands, Tolly became visibly more nervous. He could hardly eat or sleep. He stared at nothingness for long periods. The others were concerned about him and tried to either distract or console him, with little apparent effect. When he spoke it was in a downcast manner. "Pore ol' Tom. He was such a good feller."

"And a damn good cook. I sure got spoilt with his cookin' in the short time he was with us," Bill added. "You boys cain't cook worth a shit."

"That's jist it. He was with us such a short time. Then he got kilt. And Wash. Wash got kilt even quicker'n Tom." Tolly was getting more depressed.

John the Baptist said, "It's the Lord's will. Tom *and* Wash."

"John the Baptist, you need to widen out yer damn thinkin'. With you everthing that happens is God's will." Bill's tone bordered on exasperation.

Caleb tried to change the subject. "Wadn't it purty back there in that valley? Wish we could of stayed there a while."

"It was so peaceful," said Tolly dreamily. "Reminds me of back home. Wonder if I'm ever gonna git back home? Be with Sally agin. Tom wanted to git back home. Talked about it. Well, he won't be goin' home agin.

Leastways not alive. Wonder if I'll be goin' back home to Sally in a box."

"Dammit, Tolly, you're makin' me feel lower'n a snake's ass, boy!" cried Bill.

Tolly sulked. Caleb said, "Bill, don't be too hard on 'im. None a us is married, so we don't have no idee jist how hard it'd be to have to be away from a wife."

"Bullshit! You got a gal back home that you been a-doin' the same thing with as Tolly's been a-doin' with his wife. And I don't hear you belly-achin' and cry-babyin' and goin' on and on about bein' kilt. I say Tolly needs to stand tall and be a man and take his chances jist like the rest of us. Hell yes he may git kilt. So might me or you or John the Baptist or the Sarge or General Hood or anybody. But I don't see no damn sense in havin' that the one and only thing as ever gits talked about or thought about. I say that we is all gonna die sometime, and maybe it'll be today or next week or maybe not 'til we're a hunderd. But the *talkin'* about it...."

They were all silent for a long time. Finally it was Tolly who said, "Bill, what you say makes sense. Maybe I been too keen about....you know. I'll try to be a little more chipper from now on."

* * *

Ahead the sounds of fighting were unmistakable. Artillery boomed, then crashed among the trees and fields; the pop-pop-pop-pop of musketry washed over them in waves. Some men hurried forward, others rearward. Orders were shouted. Horses, carrying men or pulling artillery field-pieces, whinnied.

A civilian, having abandoned his plow, was perched on a rail fence, straining to partake of the martial drama unraveling before him. He did not see or hear the gun being hauled up behind him, detached from its team of mules, pointed toward the Federal lines, and loaded. When it was fired the startled farmer fell backwards off the fence, unharmed but embarrassed. None of them had ever seen John the Baptist laugh so hard; he fell to the earth, clutching his sides, and rolled around for several minutes. Bill, Eli, and Caleb were laughing too, as much at their companion as at the farmer. Only Tolly seemed not amused.

The withdrawing Yankees had cut down hundreds of trees and these impeded the Southern advance, as intended. Other brigades were ordered ahead of the Texans, and they moved off cockily, promising to break the Union defenses ahead of them. The Texans waited, hearing men walking into a hail of Yankee lead, seeing the woods ahead of them getting dimmer as the smoke from thousands of fired muskets accumulated into a near-solid wall. Then the stretcher-bearers began to emerge from the chaos bearing the wounded, some of whom were crying pitifully, others suffering in silence or too shocked to feel their own pain; or unconscious; or dead. Many wounded lurched back under their own power. They saw one man whose left arm was gone almost to the shoulder. Another was dragging a badly-mauled leg and foot. A third was holding his jaw, the cheek having been shot away to reveal teeth covered with blood.

Then the unwounded came, at first in a trickle, soon in a tide. "It cain't be did, they's too many of 'em, the

Yankee position's too strong, they're in ditches, acrosst a crick, with abatis in front; it cain't be did!"

The Texans were formed into line of battle, bayonets fixed. Word was passed down the line that they were to hold their fire until they were at the enemy's trenches; Hood himself would walk them there. Then the advance began with a Rebel yell. It was not easy picking their way through the dead and wounded, the bloated horses, the smashed caissons, the wrecked wagons, the felled trees, the smoke. Everywhere the wounded implored them for water, for aid, just for attention. One wounded man grabbed Caleb by the trouser leg; he had been hit in the crotch and his genitals had been blown away. He begged Caleb to shoot him. Caleb shook his head. Then he begged Caleb to cut his throat or bayonet him; Caleb, reluctantly, heartsick, walked on.

All around them bullets were thudding into trees and into men. Some of them went down silently, dead before they hit the ground. Others screamed or moaned or just uttered expletives.

Colonel Marshall was the only officer on horseback, making an inviting target, and some anonymous Yankee accommodated him, shooting him in the head fatally.

A white blur passed Caleb going forward. It was Candy, a little terrier belonging to an officer in another company. Caleb wondered fleetingly, what would induce a dog to charge into this den of death? Did it imagine that there were Yankee dogs ahead that needed attacking?

Then they were splashing across a creek. The noise was unbelievable: deafening, constant, terrible. Through the pointed abatis they picked their way, and there were the Yankee trenches! Again the Rebel yell, *now* they could shoot at last. Leveled bayonets sprang at the Yankees, some of whom began to vacate their trenches. More Texans arrived, more Yankees fled, and soon the position had been entirely overrun. Among the prizes were a score or more of Federal artillery pieces.

They had time to catch their breath and take a pull from their canteens and survey the scene. Dead and wounded men of both persuasions were everywhere, and the sight was heart-rending, the smell of smoke and feces and urine suffocating. But to Caleb the saddest thing in life at that moment was the sight of the little dead Candy, laying a few feet in front of the Northern trench, a canine sacrifice to the Southern cause. A dozen feet away, also dead, was Candy's master.

Suddenly there was heavy firing off on the flank. "It's Yankee cavalry!" They formed up and began to fire, mostly at sounds. The woods were so thick and the lingering smoke so heavy that few bluecoats could actually be seen. Ten minutes later this threat had been repulsed, and they sank exhausted to the ground. It was dusk, and word was passed that they would stay there. "Eat rations if you've got 'em, and sleep where you are. Tomorrow we'll bury the dead."

* * *

Caleb had nightmares. All night he re-fought the battle. The wounded and dead assumed the faces of his friends. There had not been time to locate anyone.

Next morning he found Bill, then Eli, then Tolly. "Where is John the Baptist?" No one had seen him.

They were put to work burying corpses. Having been dead for hours, they were stiff. Some had died in such grotesque postures that it was impossible to bury them in the traditional way. None of the graves was very deep; the sheer number of dead obviated doing the job properly.

Then they had time to talk. "I sure hope John the Baptist is alright," said a concerned Caleb.

"That was some fight. We give them Yankees a good lickin', didn't we?" Eli was exhausted but elated.

Bill said, "I never seen so many dead folks, ner wounded neither."

Tolly had said nothing the entire day. Finally Eli said, "Tolly, you ain't said nary a word. What's on yer mind, boy?"

Tolly blanched. "I guess you boys don't know, do you?"

"Know what?"

"It's the captain. He went down right next to me. He was hit real bad, right in the belly." He had to pause to regain his control. "I stopped and bent over him. His eyes was all wild-lookin'. He looked down and seen how bad he was hit, and he says 'Momma!' and then he jist died. I seen him die!"

*   *   *

It started to rain, and the shallow graves began to yield up their gruesome contents.

*   *   *

As they marched toward Richmond they passed a field hospital. A blind soldier, hysterical, was running amok among the tents, screaming "I cain't see!", finally falling over a rope. Just as they were about to get clear of the hospital area they heard a familiar voice. "Boys! Wait up!" It was John the Baptist. "The Lord spared me. Jist a little nick on my arm."

Chapter 12

▼

The Dallas **Spectator** July 4, 1862

Richmond is saved! After seven days of some of the most severe fighting North America has ever witnessed, McClellan's hordes have been repulsed. Joe Johnston has been wounded and succeeded by Robert E. Lee, so it seems one talented general has been replaced by another. Our Texas Brigade under Hood was most instrumental in throwing the Federals back, fighting with distinction at Gaines' Mill. Unfortunately, Colonel John Marshall lost his life. Yankees are clearly no match for Southern valor!

*   *   *

They camped near Richmond for a month. Some of them attended Colonel Marshall's funeral, including Sergeant Trammell. John the Baptist rejoined them a week after the battle. "I rilly hated that hospital. All them pore boys havin' arms and legs cut off. And the piles of legs and arms.... You ain't ever seen nothin' like it."

They got a new captain named Hamilton. And they finally got a replacement for Tom, Benjamin Larkin. Ben was older and quiet. He had been a carpenter back in Texas. "Good. When winter comes and we build us a new hut you'll be handier than a pocket on a shirt," cried Eli.

"Maybe the war will be over before next winter and we will be home," said an unconvinced Tolly. He was still a source of deep concern to his comrades. He slept badly when at all and was eating next to nothing. Whenever he got a letter from his wife he would look even sadder, and was observed crying after reading one of them. He wrote to her almost every day now. Bill tried to get him to go with him to the whorehouse. "You don't have to do nothin', jist *go* with me. I got money this time."

"Naw, you go ahead on, Bill. I don't care nothin' about it."

"So you're jist gonna moon around and waste away, is that yer plan?"

"Don't have no plan. Sure do wish I could go home and see Sal."

He applied for furlough but was turned down. "True, we've driven the Yankees away from Richmond for now, but they're still down the peninsula and we can certainly expect a new push any time, so we can't spare you, Johnson," said Captain Hamilton.

Camp life was leisurely. They resumed many of the activities of the winter: outdoor games, card-playing, band concerts. Passes into Richmond were issued frequently. Sutlers began to make almost daily visits to camp, including the one they had nearly cleaned out. He recognized some of them but seemed to be in a let-bygones-be-bygones mood. "Boys, jest to show you I don't bear you no hard feelins, I'm gonna let you have some of my special sausage at half price." They jumped at the bargain and bought six rolls.

That night they cooked the first one. As they began to eat it they found an inordinate amount of waste. Fingers went into mouths and fished out larger and larger pieces of gristle, then bone, then fur, teeth, ears, and claws. "Y'all know what that dirty son of a bitch has did? He's ground up cats and sold it to us fer sausage!" Bill was furious. John the Baptist, who spat out his share of the bogus concoction, was more philosophical. "Serves us right. It's our punishment fer the stealin' was done to him before."

"But you never stole nothin', John the Baptist. Why should *you* be punished fer somethin' *we* done?" asked Caleb.

"He who lies down with dogs must share their fleas."

They went to see Bill Hamman, now commissary sergeant. "Not much I can do, boys. After all, by your own admission you had stolen quite a bit from him. Just don't trade with him any more."

*   *   *

They were wakened by a heart-stopping scream. It was Tolly. He was sitting up on his bed, sweating, his eyes large and rolling around in their sockets. "What's the matter, Tolly?" asked a solicitous Caleb.

There was no reply, only an uncomprehending stare. Eli lit a lamp and put a soothing hand on Tolly's shoulder; Tolly stared at him as if at a stranger. Bill asked, "Was you havin' another bad dream?" Still no answer. Finally John the Baptist sat on Tolly's bed and took his hand. "It's gonna be alright, Tolly."

"It ain't gonna be alright. We been a-killin' folks, and it says in the Bible that thou shalt not kill, and yer sins will be found out, and that the wages a sin is death."

"But the Good Book also says that the Lord is a man of war, Tolly. Sometimes we have to fight wars. Think about all the Bible heroes that fought, like David and Joshua and Samuel and a whole raft more. Besides, you ain't kilt nobody that you're sure about, has you?"

Tolly did not reply, instead resuming his stare at nobody and nothing in particular. John the Baptist continued, "What was you dreamin', Tolly?"

"I dreamed that I was shot in the head and it made me blind. Then I went home and Sally would take me out on the streets and we would beg fer money. And then Sal, she got tired a that and she run off and left me jist a-standin' there in the dark. Then I woke up."

"No wonder. That's a *real* bad dream, Tolly. But none a that ain't a-gonna happen. You ain't gonna git blind, and even if you was to, Sally wouldn't go off and leave you. She's yer wife and she loves you. Don't she write you all the time?" Tolly looked at John the Baptist as if he really wanted to believe him.

Caleb asked, "Tolly, do you want to try and go back to sleep now?"

"Naw, I don't think so. I'm gonna go out and walk around some." He took his musket with him.

Ben slept through all of this.

*   *   *

Two mornings later Tolly reported for sick call. "What's the matter?" Eli wanted to know.

"My knee is all swole up."

"Don't look swole up to me. Do it hurt?"

"Yeah." He took his musket with him.

"You boys notice how Tolly has been takin' his piece with him wherever he goes, even to pee?" Eli asked.

"I think he's jist about to go crazy as a bed-bug," Bill opined.

The next morning at sick call Tolly reported a stomach ache. "I ain't shit in two weeks."

"You don't eat enough to keep a ant alive, so no wonder you ain't shittin'," said Bill.

The following day Tolly indicated he was again going on sick call. "Now what?" exclaimed a clearly unsympathetic Bill.

"See this cut on my finger? Don't it look to you boys like it's gittin' infected?"

"Not really."

After he left Caleb said, "John the Baptist, what do you make of Tolly?"

"The boy is in real trouble. I worry about him and pray about him all the time. Speakin' a prayin', I woke up the other night and he was on his knees a-prayin', which ordinarily I would say was a good sign. I jist wish some a you boys would do some of it. But in Tolly's case...."

Ben spoke rarely, but he did now. "Next time we go into a fight, that boy'll light out."

*   *   *

They had time to mend their tattered clothing. Out of necessity each of them had become proficient with a needle and thread. But the best was Eli. He could sew on a button faster and better than most women any of them knew. Bill teased him. "Old Romeo here is gonna make some lucky person a wonderful wife."

John the Baptist said, "Eli, I kin sew buttons on, but they keep comin' off. I've got this special button that belonged to my Granddaddy that I'm gonna ast you to sew on my pocket, because I sure as heck wouldn't wanta lose it. Would you do it?"

"Sure, lemme have it. Say, how come it's red?"

"I'm not sure. I think it was offa some uniform or other a his."

"Gonna look awful funny, a red button on yer gray tunic."

The sergeant agreed. "Martin, that button don't match yer uniform, boy."

"I know, Sarge, but my Grandmaw sent it to me in the mail. She said my Granddaddy's last wish was that I wear his button on my uniform. It's like a symbol a his soul is a-goin' into battle with me, helpin' to whup the Yankees."

The sergeant reflected on this for a moment. "Well, I guess it won't hurt nothin'. We wouldn't want to do nothin' to disappoint yer Grandpaw's soul, now would we?"

Caleb asked, "Did yer Grandmaw really tell you that story about the button?"

"No."

"Why John the Baptist, I've never knowed you to tell a lie about nothin'."

"It's jist a little white lie."
"More like a red one," said Ben.

*   *   *

Caleb found a note on his bed marked Personel. He took it outside and read it in privacy.

"You are a lier, you told me you havnet sed nuthin to no boddy about me but I know you have. Ever time I see Toly go pis or where ever he gos he takes his gun with him and I know it to shoot me with. Also the other boys looks at me funy so I am quiet sure you have told them about me. You know what happens to liers. One of these days or nites when all your smart frends arnt aroud something bad is going to happen to you Mr. Lier. I thogt that you was my frend you let me hep you but now I know you are just a rat and a snake. You think you are so pretty and such a good sojer and all the time tring to be so dam good and has a gal back home that is just a coten pikker and nuthin speshel but probly just fucks you ever time you wants it. You beter wach out Boy because I am getting tared of your face."

Caleb did not tell anyone of this. For the next several nights his sleep was fretful.

Chapter 13

The Dallas **Spectator,** August 12, 1862

One of the most brilliant leaders to emerge for our Southern cause has been Thomas J. Jackson, who has earned the sobriquet "Stonewall". His victories in the Shenandoah Valley against overwhelming odds have awed the world. When the war broke out this quiet, religious man was teaching mathematics at the Virginia Military Institute. He is a wondrous example of manhood arising to the defense of liberty.

*   *   *

They were off campaigning again, with light marching orders: three days rations, mostly hard tack, no tents, no surplus clothing. They had to work hard to keep Tolly up with them. Whenever they would stop for a break or a meal or the night, he would be like an obstinate child to prod into resuming the march.

They camped near a corn field. Several of them went into the field to gather some of the still-green corn, and to their amazement encountered a bunch of Yankees doing the same thing. None of them had come armed, so there ensued an engagement that began as a cuss-fight, then a series of fistfights and wrestling matches punctuated by men throwing ears of corn at each other. The commotion attracted others, and the outnumbered Yankees fled with curses and threats. The green corn was cooked and the men ate their fill. Some of them ate too much and were afflicted with diarrhea. The next day when the march was resumed it was not uncommon to see men discard their britches to facilitate hurried defecation; a few others took knives or bayonets and cut the seats out of their trousers. For weeks they would talk of the "roasting ears fight".

The brigade was ordered to clear a pass or "gap" that was held by the Yankees. The action opened with federal artillery firing at the forming Texans. Tolly immediately went white at the first exploding shell. Then they were ordered to advance and capture the position. Tolly froze.

"Come on, Tolly, let's go!" Caleb implored him.

"Johnson, git movin'!" shouted Sergeant Trammell. But Tolly dropped his piece and turned and ran to the rear. "No, Tolly, don't!" screamed John the Baptist. "You got to help us!" It was to no avail. He disappeared into the woods.

They had no time to dwell on Tolly's defection. Ahead was death in the form of the Union batteries, which had to be silenced. They fixed bayonets and charged with their Rebel yell. Not only shells but also minie balls took their toll of the Texans. Ben went down; Bill, Eli, John the Baptist, and Caleb re-doubled their efforts, as if to make up for his absence plus that of the cowardly Tolly. Just ahead of them, 20 yards away, was a Yankee fieldpiece. Suddenly all the blue-coated gunners turned and fled, all except an officer, who kept loading and firing alone. He was quickly shot down by the Southerners. They went to the prostrate captain and saw that he was very badly hit, in the shoulder and chest. "Sir, we'll take you to our hospital, it ain't but about a mile or two from here."

"No, boys, thank you anyhow for your kindness. But I think I'm hurt too bad to move. Just let me stretch out here and get my breath."

He was bleeding heavily, and his breathing became more uneven. Within minutes he was dead. The Texans removed their scraggly hats and stood over him for a few minutes in silence, then buried him next to the piece he had served so faithfully and so fatally. John the Baptist prayed over his grave.

* * *

Next day Ben was with them. "Ball jist knocked me down. Hardly felt it, rilly. Had a letter in my pocket from my sister and that took mosta the blow." He took out the letter, which looked like a handful of confetti.

"Sure hope you'd read that sucker already," said Eli.

A huge battle was shaping up to the east. Division after division was maneuvering and marching. The sounds of thousands of men engaged in combat emanated from the middle distance. Then they were pointed toward the field of Mars.

"Reckon we'll ever git used to it, goin' into battle?" Caleb asked Bill.

"Not me, fool. What I'd like to git used to is goin' home and gittin' drunk and toppin' me a differnt gal ever night."

"You don't ast much outa life, do you Bill?" said Eli.

"Now I know you boys'd ruther be here than anywheres else," Ben grinned.

"Wish that damned Tolly hadn't lit out," John the Baptist thus shocked all of them.

Then they were too occupied to talk anymore.

In their front were the New York Zouaves with their red shirts and baggy pants, whom they recalled from the confrontation on the frozen Potomac of the winter previous. The sight of them was like the proverbial red shirt being waved before the bull. The remembered taunts spurred the Texans forward in a fierce, irresistible charge, the Rebel yell issuing from thousands of throats with a fervor unequaled in the war. The Zouaves wavered, then fell back, then fled in panic. Many of them were shot down, some were bayoneted, hundreds surrendered. One Zouave jumped into a creek which quickly filled his baggy pants with water, and he emerged on the far bank looking for all the world like a man wearing heavy balloons for trousers. Bill and Eli shot at him, puncturing his pants with holes that spurted water as if from a sieve. Caleb and John the Baptist stopped firing and just had a good laugh. Encumbered as he was with water, leaking though it was, the Yankee was forced to throw down his piece and raise his hands in surrender.

When the battle was over the elated Texans had captured three of the enemy's colors.

* * *

The sergeant said, "Boys, I need....no, General Hood needs some volunteers." John the Baptist, then Eli, then Caleb, and finally Bill stepped forward. They were joined by a dozen others, including a sullen Henry Dowd. "Boys, there are some Yankee ambulances the other side of that stand of trees, and General Hood would admire to have them."

They set off through the trees. Occasionally Caleb would cast a sidelong glance at Henry, who invariably was looking at him through narrowed slits in a fashion calculated to appear hostile and threatening. But neither spoke to the other.

The three ambulances were guarded by only a half dozen infantrymen, and they and the teamsters quickly surrendered to the Texans. The vehicles were proudly driven to General Hood's headquarters, where a beaming Hood thanked them. Suddenly a staff officer rode up. "General Hood, General Longstreet requests that these ambulances be turned over to your superior, General Evans, at once, sir."

"I'll be damned if I will, sir," replied an enraged Hood. "My boys captured them, not General Evans's boys. Besides, it was my intention to present them to General Lee with my compliments."

The staff officer rode off. The men took their ease, smoking and drinking from their canteens. A half hour later the staff officer returned. "General Hood, General Longstreet presents his compliments and directs me to tell you that you are under arrest for refusing to obey his orders."

The Texans picked up their pieces and shot threatening glances at the staff officer. Hood, sensing a situation that could easily get out of hand very fast, said to the men, "Boys, just stand easy. I'll ride over to General Longstreet and straighten this out."

Caleb said, "It don't seem right, we capture them and General Evans gits 'em."

"I been tellin' y'all that these Goddamn people don't know shit from sawdust," Bill announced.

They went back to their units, where they later learned that Hood's arrest had been suspended by General Lee, but that he had been relieved of command temporarily. There was talk of mutiny but the officers and non-coms quelled it quickly. "That ain't the way to help the general, it'll only hurt 'im. Make it look like he can't control his people." So the furor died.

And they heard that Tolly was in the guard house.

* * *

The guard unlocked the barred door and let Caleb in. Tolly looked terrible: hair disheveled, tear stains on dirty cheeks, clothes little more than rags.

"I'm glad to see you, Caleb. Thanks fer comin'. I figgered none a you would want to have nothin' to do with me since I lit out."

"Shucks, Tolly, you oughtn't to think that. We all likes you, always has ever since we all left Texas together. The others was too busy to come," he lied.

"I jist couldn't take it no more. It wasn't that I was so skeered. Well, I *was* skeered, but that ain't all of it. I jist kept gittin' all them letters from Sally about how much she missed me, how much she worried about somethin' happenin' to me, me maybe comin' home a cripple. But then that last letter...." His voice trailed away, and he sobbed.

"What did she say, Tolly?"

When his composure returned in a few moments, Tolly went on. "She said that one a her cousins was comin' after her, you know, tryin' to git her to be with him...." Again he broke. Caleb stepped over and put a reassuring hand on his shoulder.

"Well, it was jist more than I could stand. I know that Sal ain't never been with no other man 'cept me, and the thought a that big plug-ugly...." Again he wept, this time sinking to the floor. "So I had to try to git to her, to pertect her from that bastard."

Caleb shook his head ever so slightly. "So that was it. We wondered what caused you to take off." He reflected. "Tolly, anybody kin unnerstand that."

"No they cain't. I ran! I deserted you boys! I'm a coward. It don't matter why. And do you think Sarge will unnerstand? Or the captain? Or General Hood or anybody else? Look at me! I'm in a military prison, a deserter. I could be shot! Even if I ain't shot, I am disgraced." His aspect was one of total despondency.

"Tolly, I know you feel bad. But you ain't the only one who has ever ran."

"But you ain't ran, Caleb."

"No, but I've felt like it."

"Really? When?"

"Lotsa times. You see, Tolly...." He had to decide if he wanted to tell Tolly about his Problem. After another minute's hesitation he concluded that the stakes were high enough to divulge his Secret.

"Tolly, here we are fightin' a war to keep slavery, and I think slavery is wrong." He waited for this information to sink into his friend's consciousness a bit, then he proceeded. "My Poppa don't have no slaves. There ain't but one slave anyplace clost to us and that is Quince, the Sammons's nigger, and he is one a the best men I know. He is smart, he is honest, he is a hard worker, he has showed me how to do a bunch a things that even my own Poppa didn't show me, like how to gentle a mean mule. If I could I would set Quince free. And yet here I am up here a-fightin' to keep him a slave. And all the way up here from Texas we seen slaves bein' mistreated. That upsets me. If I think about it too much *I* might light out."

Tolly was thoughtful for a long time. "Caleb, sometimes this world is too crazy. Here is me and you up here in the army, away from home, me away from a wife that needs me, you a-fightin' fer to keep a good man a slave....I don't know, sometimes I jist don't know."

The guard yelled in the door, "Time's up!"

"Tolly, you take care a yerself. It's gonna be alright. I'll tell the boys why you ran and they'll unnerstand."

"Thanks, Caleb. I'm glad you came. I feel better now."

* * *

Next morning Bill said, "Did you boys hear? Tolly hung hisself last night."

Chapter 14

▼

The Dallas **Spectator,** September 9, 1862

Another glorious victory for General Lee and the Army of Northern Virginia! On the old Manassas Battlefield our gallant forces defeated the arrogant Pope, who reportedly had vowed to show the Army of the Potomac how Westerners won victories; McClellan must have taken secret pleasure in Pope's failure. Again our Texas Brigade was in the van, by its brave example.

* * *

Sergeant Trammell was more animated than they had ever seen him. "Sarge, you look like you jist swallered a giggle-bug. What's up?"

"We're goin' to go up North. Goin' to invade the enemy's country. Fight on his ground fer awhile."

But not all of them went. Ben had had a setback from his wound; it was bruised and very sore, so he was detached to guard duty. Eli had come down with the fever and was in the hospital.

As they headed for the Potomac Tolly was much on their minds. "I guess his pore soul has gone to hell since he took his own life," John the Baptist mused out loud.

"That seems awful harsh to me," said Caleb. "Looks like a forgivin' God would take into account how tormented he was, about his wife and all."

"The boy was a damn coward, that's the long and the short of it. We're well rid of 'im, I says." Bill said it with the finality of the Last Judgement. "*We've* got to fight, so why shouldn't he? Wife er no wife. And he did join up. Nobody held a gun on 'im."

"Some people is made tougher than others. Jist like some kin work longer and harder than others. Why, my little brother Jamie, he's five years younger than me, and he kin work circles aroun' me."

"But Caleb, we are all in this together. We're like a chain. If there is one weak link, the whole chain has gotta break. If Tolly or anybody else is weak, we are all in danger. And what about the Cause? There ain't no way we kin win if you've got very many Tollys lightin' out."

"John the Baptist is right. Man like Tolly gits me and you kilt, Caleb. He runs, that's one less to stand up and face the Yankees. I'd favor shootin' the bastards soon as they show their ass to the enemy."

"Speakin' a which, I heard an interstin' story the other day from one a the boys that guards General Lee," Caleb told them. "I don't know if you've saw him er not, but there's a English colonel that's been with General Lee as a observer, and the other day he says to General Lee, 'Ain't you disgraced by the ragged look a them Texans? Why, some of 'em even has the ass outa their pants.' And General Lee, he says, 'Colonel, never mind the raggedness a my Texans, the enemy never sees their backs.' I thought that made a good story."

*   *   *

As they crossed into Maryland the morale of the army was elevated. There was a general feeling that the war had entered a new phase. Thus far they had been parrying the thrusts of the enemy, reacting to his moves. Now let *him* do the parrying for a while; we have the initiative. Victory will be ours, and it will be won in the North.

*   *   *

Many things in his 20 years had surprised Caleb, but none more than the chilly reception the army received in Maryland. He and his comrades had understood that Maryland was a Southern state, where the "peculiar institution" was legal. True, Maryland had not seceded, but had that not been because of high treachery by her officials and quick action by the Federal army? Caleb had heard stories about Baltimore citizens attacking Yankee soldiers on their way south to Washington. Thus the sullen farmers and unfriendly townfolk in Maryland were a shock.

The column was halted at a farm and Caleb, Bill, and John the Baptist dropped their haversacks and cartridge boxes under a tree. Bill saw the well a few yards away and started for it when a woman emerged from the house carrying a rolling pin. Her wrinkled face was livid. "I'll thank you Rebel scum to leave my water be!"

Bill reddened. "Ma'am, I've been raised up to respect womenfolk, 'specially old womenfolk, but if you don't let us have some water to drink, I reckon I'm gonna fergit my manners and jist kick this ol' well in."

"It's jest like you Rebel riff-raff to sass a pore ol' lone woman. Why, if my boys was here you wouldn't be so smart-mouth. They'd learn you some manners."

"Ma'am, we ain't astin' fer yer daughters, or even fer no food. All we want is jist a little water fer to wet our dry throats. It ain't gonna cost you nothin'."

"It'll cost me havin' my well polluted."

Bill drew a bucket of water, drank deeply, then filled his canteen and those of Caleb and John the Baptist. When he returned to his mates he muttered, "I ought to shit in that ol' lady's well."

"Now Bill, have a little Christian charity fer that pore misguided old soul," said John the Baptist soothingly.

Caleb offered, "I guess she don't see us as no liberators."

Bill laughed. "I s'pose if we had horns we wouldn't look no worser to her."

* * *

They had walked most of the night and were famished. From up ahead the sounds of fighting were becoming clearer, with artillery and musketry rolling across the land in the waves that they had become so familiar with. Word came down the line that, at last, they could cook rations.

"Goddamn, it's about time. My belly thinks my throat has been cut," Bill exclaimed.

"Bill, the Lord is keeping a register of all these blasphemies you are uttering. The day of reckoning will be hard for you."

"Bullshit, John the Baptist. Let the Lord take better care a me, send me some good food, a new pair a shoes, a juicy young virgin. Then I'll sing his praises so loud you'll be beggin' me to shut up so you kin git some sleep."

"I worry about your immortal soul when you talk like that."

"Worry about that bacon yer s'posed to be watchin'. It's about to burn up. That's gonna taste so much better'n them worm castles they call hardtack."

Caleb said, "Don't that smell good? How long has it been since we et bacon? A good week, I know."

The sergeant shouted, "Boys, we are needed! Give me a column right here."

"That makes me so Goddamn mad I cain't see straight!" Bill screamed. "These officers don't know shit from holy water. First they tell us to cook, then they order us to move out."

"I'd much ruther eat than fight, but I don't reckon we've got no choice," Caleb said.

They passed a white-washed church and began to enter a field of shoulder-high corn when a hail of bullets such as none of them had experienced began to assail them. Immediately they began to take casualties. Their officers ordered them to charge. As they went further into the cornfield, the men encountered a hideous sight: there were Georgians and Louisianans by the hundreds lying on the ground, some dead, some wounded in the most horrible fashion. Caleb saw one man with his left arm severed at the elbow and resting inches from where its owner, still alive, was crying and reaching for the detached member with his good arm. Another had the top of his head blown away. A third was sitting amidst the corn calmly trying to push his protruding entrails back into his midsection. Caleb knew better than to stop and offer any succor. Bill was on his left and John the Baptist on his right as they kept advancing. It would have been wholly possible to walk only on the bodies of the dead and wounded if they had chosen. The smoke from muskets and the few fires that the battle had caused among the cornstalks was making it harder to see and breathe as they pressed on.

Then Caleb heard a noise that sounded as if someone had dropped a watermelon. John the Baptist was down. Caleb stopped and knelt over his friend. John the Baptist was lying on his back, his face gone. What remained was a mixture of blood, bone, brains, and teeth all jumbled together in a skull that angled obscenely to one side. The corpse was emptying its bowels and its bladder. The only way Caleb could tell that this macabre being was John the Baptist was that the gray tunic bore the incongruous red button on the left pocket. Caleb stifled a sob. It was obvious that he could not help his friend. He stood up, about to resume his advance, when he saw General Hood himself on horseback dimly through the smoke. He was shouting, "Go back, boys! Go back!" Caleb looked around for Bill but could not locate him. He retreated.

Back at camp all was chaos. Wounded were everywhere, bleeding and moaning. As the hours passed Caleb became more concerned about Bill. Finally, at dusk, Bill appeared, a blood-soaked bandage around his right arm. "I was real worried about you. Are you bad hurt?"

"It ain't bad, jist a scratch, really. Missed the bone. Where is John the Baptist?"

"He's dead, Bill. Got hit right in the face. I doubt he felt a thing."

Bill looked genuinely distressed. After a minute of staring at the ground he said, "Well, I hope the pore bastard is at least with God."

*   *   *

Next day they began to retreat back to Virginia. When they came to the farm of the woman who had begrudged them the water, Bill kicked in her well.

Chapter 15

The Dallas **Spectator**, September 30, 1862

General Lee has made a foray into Maryland, with the intent of replenishing his supplies and recruiting Southern sympathizers. His efforts seem to have been not altogether successful, as the Army of Northern Virginia had to retreat back across the Potomac. The sharp engagement at Sharpsburg was once again spearheaded by the Texas Brigade, but reports are that the enemy was too great in its numbers to allow for Confederate success.

* * *

They crossed the Potomac glumly, in sharp contrast to the jaunty crossing going the other way. The army had been badly mauled, and none more than the Texans.

"They say we won the battle up there," Caleb said.

"If that's winnin', I'd sure as hell hate to be in one we lost," was Bill's retort. "And if'n we won, how come we're goin' back to Virginia?"

They remained in the lovely Shenandoah Valley for five weeks, recuperating. They got new uniforms, and their spiffy look helped to raise their morale damaged by the loss of so many comrades. Caleb dreamed often of John the Baptist, and one night woke up crying after dreaming that John the Baptist was not really dead, that a mistake had been made. He wondered who back in Texas would mourn his friend. "Will Liz have to mourn for me? Will I survive this war?"

Hood was promoted to major general and given the division. Sergeant Trammell had mixed emotions about this. "Glad to see him bein' reconized, but hate to lose him as the brigade commander. Higher up he gits, less we're likely to see of 'im."

"Who is the new commander a the brigade?" Caleb asked.

"Colonel Robertson. Well, I guess he's General Robertson now. He's back from recuperatin'. He done good with the regiment; let's see how he can handle the brigade."

*   *   *

Ben joined them. "Where's Eli?" they asked.

"Eli died a the fever."

"I don't unnerstant that," said a perplexed Caleb. "Most a the ones that the fever carried off was last fall and winter. Ain't been much of it this summer." They all shook their heads in consternation, as if Eli had played a dirty trick on them.

A big parade was held. They passed in review before Generals Lee, Longstreet, and Hood. Out of the corners of their eyes they could see elegant ladies on horseback watching them, which put extra spring in their step. "I bet we look good," whispered Caleb to Bill beside him.

"I'd ruther one a them purty ladies could see me without *no* clothes on, jist me an' her."

"Bill, you'd make a dog laugh."

They moved to the old camp at Fredericksburg, where they had been in the spring. The Georgia regiment that had been with them from the beginning was detached and replaced by the Third Arkansas. It was not that they had disliked the Georgians, but they seemed to have more in common with the Arkansans. They could understand each other better for one thing. There were fights, of course, but fewer than before.

It was starting to get colder. Each succeeding morning their breath was more apparent, and then one morning a thin layer of ice covered the water in their wash buckets. All the leaves had fallen from the deciduous trees.

They drilled constantly and pulled much picket duty. Also they constructed earthworks, especially on the heights behind the town. The Yankees were across the river in great force, and it seemed reasonable that soon they would come over and assault the Southerners.

"Sergeant, kin that river be forded?" asked Caleb.

"Naw, boy, too deep. They'll have to build bridges acrosst it, pontoons most likely."

"Cain't we keep 'em from doin' that, with artill'ry and small arms?"

"In any artill'ry duel, they'll likely come out ahead. They got more and better. As fer the small arms, their big guns won't let us git clost enough fer that."

"When do you think they'll try it?"

"Don't know, boy. But when they do, a helluva lot of 'em is gonna die. Even if they git acrosst the river, don't see how they'll ever make it up these heights with us a-shootin' at 'em."

Winter was closing in fast, but they were not permitted to build huts. "Yankee assault is expected any day; we need to be alert for that."

    *   *   *

After weeks of tense waiting, the Federals began to build their pontoon bridges. The Southern guns could only slow this effort and inflict casualties. With the bridges finished, the Northern army was drawn up by corps across the Rappahannock. The Texans had the best seat in the house, occupying the center of the Confederate lines along the heights.

"Goddamn, have you ever saw so many men in yer life?" Bill exclaimed. "Must be a million of 'em!"

"And ever one of 'em is comin' straight fer us," Ben added.

The Yankees poured across the bridges and into the town. Then they fanned out toward the flanks and began ascending the heights. There was fierce fighting on both sides of them but the Texans essentially were excluded from the battle. This time they were allowed the luxury of watching others fight. And a grand spectacle it was. Despite their bravery, despite their greater numbers, the Yankees simply could not overcome the Southern defenses. Again and again they charged, only to be repulsed with horrible losses. The Texans wondered at their courage. "Don't them Yankees know they cain't do it? Why don't they give it up before ever last one of 'em is dead?"

At long last the Federals withdrew. As they retreated through Fredericksburg the Rebels came out of their entrenchments and harried them mercilessly with sharpshooters and bayonet charges. Only after they had crossed their floating bridges could they feel safe.

Now the Southern burial parties went to work. But before they could perform their grim chores the body-strippers came, some civilian and some military. Clothing, jewelry, personal effects were taken. Many of the corpses were naked. The frozen ground made grave-digging slow, and Federal shelling made it dangerous. Many in the burial parties themselves became candidates for interment.

CHAPTER 16

The Dallas **Spectator,** December 25, 1862

Happy Yuletide news is that new units are still being organized in Texas to aid the cause. One is Ross's Brigade of Cavalry, a second is Ector's Brigade of Dismounted Cavalry. We trust these valiant men will acquit themselves as honorably as have their predecessors in Southern service.

There is another great victory to report. The Federals under Burnside have foolishly assaulted Lee at Marye's Heights at Fredericksburg, and been repulsed with horrendous losses.

Less happy news is that at Iuka, Mississippi, the Texas Third Cavalry was badly mauled. The Federal blockade is taking its toll of necessities, with medicines at the top of the list. The loss of Galveston Island was a severe blow. The high-handed tactics of the commander of the military department of Texas, General Hebert, are being increasingly resented. He has ruled that our cotton cannot be exported. If Texas and the balance of our sister states have any economic advantage, it is our cotton. Perhaps worse is his uneven application of the conscription law, and pursuant to a very few overt defiances of that law he has arbitrarily placed the entire state under martial law.

Another unhappy circumstance is the overt disloyalty of many of our citizens, especially Germans in the south of Texas. A disappointment has been the abortive attempts to establish Confederate control over New Mexico and Arizona after initial successes there.

But we face the upcoming year with optimism, confident in the rectitude of our cause and the ability of our leaders, civilian and military.

*   *   *

Jan 21, 1863
Dear Liz,

Sorry I have not wrote you sense Christmas. It is not that we been that buzy niether, just have not had no news much. We are in huts agin and its sure warmer than tints is.

We git up at sun up for role call then fixs brekfust. Some of the boys goes on sick call but not me I have not been on sick call sense 1861 and am prowd of that. I beleive some of the boys is just lazy and don't like to drill which is what we do the rest of the morning, Drill. I don't mind drill its kind of fun akchuly to do all that walking together and the Sarge is funy somtimes when we are marching he will say things like Ive saw a flok of ducks that looks beter than you boys sept at lest they can flie and you boys cant even flie.

We eat dinner and then in the after noon we police up the camp and do our wash and mind up our close and write leters like I am doing right now liz.

At night we sometimes go to the theater and sees plays I have saw Gen Lee and Gen Longstreet and Gen Hood all their. Some of the plays is sily and some is reel serous. They has reel acters and acterises and they is reel good.

There is a preacher that gives us surmons name of Davis. He is also good to visit the sick and hurt, in fact he even got us Texans are own hospital in Richmond.

Our new general is Robertson, we call him "Aunt Polly" because he takes sich good car of us, sept he missed our last fight.

The Yankees is right acrost the River in there winter camp. Sometimes we run acrost them when we go on patrole or chopin threw the ice to git water or looking for something to eat. We usally don't shoot at one another when we see them like this. Its like their is a agremint not to fight in small bunches only in big bunches. I have even talked to some of them and they don't seem like bad boys atal.

You rember I told you about Tolly who hung hisself. I don't perticlerly like what he done runing I meen but at the same time I don't agree with what some of the boys says about we are beter off with him ded. I don't think it's a mans place to say if anuther man ott to be ded or alive. Tolly had a awful amont of things on his mind like his wife writting all them sad leters and he was always worried about gitting shot and going back home a criple. He had this one dreem where he thought he was blind and he woke us all up screeming, I may have wrote you that Liz. I think its natcherul to wury about gitting shot or hurt or cripled cause I do think about such but not all the time I don't. What I use to wury about was would I run and I found out I didn't at lest so far. But ever man is difernt and some is braver (or dummer) and somtimes I am not sure I know the difernce.

I sure do miss John the Babtist you know me and him and Bill was togather from the very begining back in Texas. He was a awfull good feller and a good soljer but Liz even he got down on what Tolly done.

We got us a new man in our hut he is call Aaron and he just come up from Tex. he is green as new lumber and me and Bill and Ben is shoing him what to do speshully he don't know nothing atal about cooking cause he says his Mother wouldn't never let him in her kichen hardly even to git a drink of milk. He is a little gotch-eyed, you know his eyes sted of looking strait ahead kindly looks away from one another. Its hard to tell who he is looking at. And he is reel skeered of frogs, says when they jump it is to jurky. Bill played a trick on him, tole him to git his umbrela from the Sarge, he had a nee slapin laff. Aaron tuck it prety good. We are shorthanded with Eli gone of the fever and Tolly and John the Babtist also gone. I just hope we gits some more boys to hep with fighting them Yankees.

Its been reel cold and snows and sletes a lot but I stay warm.

Write when you can Liz as I sure so like to here from you.

Love,
Caleb

* * *

Captain Hamilton addressed his assembled company. "Men, I've been getting reports of thefts from the farmers hereabouts. They are saying that many of their pigs and chickens have been disappearing and they doubt that the animals have run away to look for better homes at nearby farms." The men snickered. "If you know of anyone who would do such a thing, kindly inform him that stealing is against the law and a violation of the Ten Commandments." He paused for effect. "Also some of the regiments camped nearby are reporting thefts from their supply tents, and even some individuals are saying that items have been stolen from them personally. I am referring most particularly to shoes, knapsacks, and skillets. It is unlikely that the enemy is doing this stealing of Confederate equipment, being better equipped than we are, so that leaves either the civilians or our own soldiers. Again let me say that if you should find out that anyone, soldier or civilian, is, has been, or is contemplating taking any items from our fellow Southern soldiers, try to use your influence on them to halt such practices. Thank you, gentlemen. Sergeant, you may dismiss the company."

"You boys remember when Captain Sealy talked to us about stealin'? Was jist about exactly a year ago and he sure took a differnt tone."

Bill said, "Caleb, me and you was the only ones here then. Ben and Aaron wasn't with us. Eli was, and John the Baptist and Tolly, they was."

"What was the differnce in tone?" Ben inquired.

"Ol' Sealy was hot as hell, red in the face, eyes bulgin' nearly outa his head," Bill replied. "I'll allow Caleb here ain't sorry to see him gone."

"What happened to 'im?" asked Aaron.

"Kilt. Gut-shot. Died right on the field. Did you do it, Caleb?"

"Course I didn't do it!"

Aaron's curiosity was up. "Why would Caleb of wanted the captain dead?"

"He was always ridin' Caleb 'bout somethin'. Anything. Everthing. None a us had no idee why."

Ben offered, "You know, it'd be awful easy to shoot somebody you didn't like in a battle. Nobody would ever know the differnce."

Caleb got very reflective. Might Henry try such a thing one of these days? Was Henry capable of cold-blooded murder? Was Henry *that* angry at me?

"Caleb, what you thinkin' about, boy? You back home with whatsername, Liz?"

"Naw, thinkin' 'bout sumpin else."

Bill continued, "I think the captain was talkin' to us about stealin' because somebody higher up tole him to. He wasn't upset or even very concerned, didn't seems to me. Fact a the binness, I thought he was downright funny. 'If you know of anyone who would do such a thing. Try to use your influence.' Hell, he ain't blind. The man kin see us walkin' around here wearin' new shoes and carryin' new knapsacks and cookin' in new skillets. He ain't a fool, he's *got* to know we been stealin' all that shit. And at least the Sarge knows we been a-stealin' chickens and pigs 'cause he sees and smells us a-cookin' 'em."

Ben added, "The Sarge knows we don't git fed enough. The commissary that don't have enough to keep *our* bellies full is the same commissary that *he* draws from, and you don't see no great fat belly a *his* a-draggin' in the dirt, does ya?"

"We throwed away so much a our stuff up in Maryland, and the goverment ain't replacin' it, and you got these here new boys that ain't been in no fights yet with all that new stuff. And we ain't been cleanin' out the farmers, we always leaves 'em *some* pigs and chickens. And ain't we a-fightin' fer them? It don't none of it seem that bad to me," Caleb said. "But I'm sure glad my Momma and Poppa cain't hear me talkin' like this 'cause I sure don't believe they'd unnerstand."

"They ain't here," Ben pointed out.

* * *

Feb. 10, 1863
My dearest Caleb,

I miss you so much. It is hard to beleive that you have been gone only a year and a half, it seems like at least ten years since we were togather. We have shared many things that married people has shared (I hope nobody but you will read this, Caleb) The idea that it could be another year and a half before I see you again makes me real sad. Let us hope that we can whip those Yankees quick and you will get to be back home with me and your family soon.

The snow fight you described sounded like great fun. I can not imagin that much snow because here it does not snow that much as you well know, Caleb.

My folks is well. My Maw had a bad coff for a few days but it is better now. So far none of the rest of us has cought it. Me and Paw has mostly been mending fences and the barn, getting ready for spring plowing in a few weeks. Rachel is in school. Margaret had a little boy last month and he is doing well. Her husband Thomas may have to go to the army.

I have been sewing a little bit this winter. That is one of the things I do not feel too good at. A wife and mother needs to be abel to sew to keep her family in clothes.

I saw your folks the other day. Your Paw is doing well and so is your Maw. You will not know Annie or David by the time you get home, Caleb. They are so big and Annie is getting real pretty with that yellow hair and blue eyes that my handsom Caleb also has. But the one that will supprise you is Jamie. He is a growed up man. You may see him before you see the others because he told me that if your Paw will let him he is going to come up and join you in Virginia. After all Jamie is 16 now and feels he needs to help out so the war can be ended and you and all the others can come home.

Caleb I have rambled on but I have tried to catch you up on the happenings here. Please take good care of yourself and come back to me soon so we can do the things we have always did.

With all my love,
Liz

Chapter 17

▼

The Dallas **Spectator,** January 22, 1863

Another unfortunate repulse, in Tennessee, at Murpheesboro; although Terry's Texas Rangers acquitted themselves bravely. Sidney Johnston is sorely missed.

Mr. Lincoln's proclamation freeing the slaves has a ridiculously hollow ring. First of all, it addresses the status of those not even under his control, and says nothing of those slaves in either the slave states that have not seceded (Delaware, Maryland, Kentucky, Missouri) or those residing in areas occupied by Federal forces (parts of Louisiana, Tennessee, Virginia, for example). Secondly, if he thinks such a bogus announcement will induce our slaves to either turn on their masters (and mistresses) or flee to "freedom", he shows a lack of understanding of our servants. There has been no recorded incident of either slave violence nor running away in the South, illustrating clearly that our colored population feels happy with the status quo. Just one more instance of wrong-headedness of this black Republican abolitionist.

But we do have Galveston Island back, thanks to General Magruder, who is such a vast improvement over Hebert.

* * *

"Fall out, boys. We are needed."

Caleb wondered if the sergeant would ever bring any variety to the order. There was the usual grumbling, especially from Bill. "Jist about the time I was gittin' to the best part a the dream, the part where I was about to stick it in her, ol' Sarge has to poke his big finger in my soap bubble."

They formed up outside the tents, shuffling and arranging their uniforms. Then the captain rode up, waited a minute until he commanded everyone's attention, and addressed them. "Boys, we got a report of Union cavalry activity to the west a ways, so we are going to form a line of skirmishers to screen off our camp just in case the Yankees have got any ideas about an attack. I know you boys will do your duty. Take them off, sergeant."

"Yessir, captain. Alright, boys, give me a column a twos and foller me."

They marched at route step for about a mile, then were halted and formed into a skirmish line facing a stand of timber. The captain commanded them, "Forward, boys, and watch sharp!"

They had gone about a hundred yards when Caleb was knocked off his feet. His first guess was that he had been kicked in the temple by a mule, except that even in his dazed state he was pretty sure that no mules were close enough to have fetched him a kick. Before he could solve the riddle, darkness closed in.

Just before he opened his eyes he could feel his head throbbing with the worst headache of his life. Instinctively his hand went up toward the source of the pain, but what he felt instead was another hand, smaller and softer, which was administering a damp cloth to his head. Then his eyes opened to a poor focus. "Liz! Liz, how did you git here to Virginia?"

"I'm not Liz, I'm Mary. Who is Liz?"

Then Caleb could see that of course it wasn't Elizabeth, that the girl's hair was longer and that she was pale, not tan like Liz was. She had said her name was Mary; maybe she was the mother of Jesus. Maybe he was dead and this was an angel who was welcoming him to heaven.

"Am I dead? Are you a angel?"

Her laugh was hearty. "My folks would *really* laugh at the suggestion that I'm an angel. No, our farm is just back there a ways. We heard the shooting, then some soldiers said there were wounded so I came out to see if I could help. You've got a little blood here on the side, and it doesn't look bad at all. I think you're going to live. What is your name?"

"Caleb, ma'am."

"You don't have to call me ma'am. I'm probably not as old as you are. How old are you, Caleb?"

"Twenty-one."

"See. I'm only eighteen. Where are you from?"

"Texas."

"My, that's a long way. It sure is generous of you Texas boys to come all the way up here to Virginia to help us."

"Yes, ma'am. I mean I guess it is, Mary. I surely do 'preciate you comin' out here to look after me. Was anybody else hurt?"

"I think one other boy was hurt in the leg. I heard one of the soldiers say that there were just a few Yankees in the woods and that they fired one volley and lit out. Are you in much pain?"

"It ain't too bad," he lied.

"Who is Liz?"

"Oh, she is this girl back home."

"Do you like her a lot?"

"Well, yes, I s'pose I do. Me and Liz has knowed one another all our lives, jist about."

"Do you write to her?"

"I'm not the best in the nation about writin', but I drop her a line ever chancet I git."

The surgeon appeared and Mary gave way. "Doesn't look too bad. Looks like this young lady has just about got the bleeding stopped. Can you stand up?"

With the help of the surgeon and Mary, Caleb stood. He was wobbly and a little dizzy, and his stomach felt queasy. "Well, I don't feel real chipper."

"Then we'll take you back in the ambulance. The other boy is already loaded."

"Who else got hit, sir?"

"I don't know his name. He has a ball lodged in his leg and I'll have to take it out back at the hospital."

Mary said, "Caleb, I have an investment in you now that I have tended to your wound, so I want to know how you are mending. Our place is the Tolbert farm. Whenever you feel up to it, why don't you come around and let me know how you are coming along?"

"That sounds like an excellent idea to me," the surgeon offered. "I'll even write out an order to that effect, that your rehabilitation will be promoted by you going over to Miss Tolbert's from time to time."

And so it was. The brigade remained in the area for a few weeks, and Caleb went to the Tolbert farm several times. Each time Mary looked at his wound and pronounced it better. And each time the conversation worked its way around to Liz Wright back home in Texas.

"Are you going to marry Liz?"

"Prob'ly. We ain't exactly talked about it but I think we both have jist figgered that it would be the natural thing to happen."

"Well, I think she is a very lucky girl."

Caleb blushed. "Mary, I think whoever marries you is gonna be lucky too. And it looks like you are gonna have the pick a the litter. Why, I've never been here that there wasn't two or three or four men and boys a-pantin' after you."

It was her turn to blush. "I don't know about that. There *are* several young men that I have tried in my small way to nurse back to health. But my Daddy says that I am too young to be receiving suitors just yet, and besides, we all need to be thinking about winning the war first."

"Yes, I absolutely agree."

*   *   *

Feb 20, 1863
Dear Elizabeth,

I am sorry I have not wrote to you in so long, but we have been awfull buzy. We have had a few sharp fights but I am fine. Well Liz, to tell the truth I did git one littel scrape on my head but it is not anything bad. What happened was this ball must of just shaved me a littel clost and I was out for a spell. When I woke up their was this beatiful girl over me with a wet rag and she was wiping my head where the scrape was at. I thought I had died and gone to heaven and this was a angle tending to me. Her name is Mary and her folks lives here on this big farm in Virginia and we have been camped clost by for a few weeks and Mary has insisted that I should go over their ever few days so she can take a look at how I am comming along. I keep telling her that we have a regimental surgin to look after us but she wont hear of it. I have even et their a few times. Sombody must be doing a good job on my scrape because it is just about gone.

Well Liz, tell your folks hello for me and also my folks if you should see them. Keep writting as I always injoy your leters so.

Love,
Caleb

*   *   *

"Pack up, boys, we're movin' south."

"However far south it is, I hope we git clear a this blizzard," Caleb said.

"Wouldn't you jist know that they'd wait 'til a damn blizzard hit to move us out? Couldn't have did it any a the last few days when the sun was a-shinin'. They don't know shit from seaweed." Bill was his usual cheerful and optimistic self.

They marched through Richmond. The snowfall had abated and a large, enthusiastic crowd cheered their progress through the city.

"Wonder why these folks likes us so much?" Caleb wondered out loud.

"Cause we're so purty?"

"Aaron, I doubt that's it," Ben chuckled.

Bill said, "What makes you think they don't holler this much fer *all* the boys as comes through here?"

"I know how to settle this. Let's jist *ast* somebody. Lady, how come y'all always gives us sech a greetin'?" Caleb had become uncharacteristically assertive.

"Why, it's because you Texans has sech a reputation as hard fighters."

Her reply was like a tonic. For the rest of the march to the camp their heads were higher and their steps springier than before.

*   *   *

"I don't have no hat," Ben announced.

"What happened to it?"

"Throwed it away. Weren't enough of it to shade a doodle-bug anyhow."

Bill got a conspiratorial look in his eyes, as if he were hatching a plot that would surely win the war. "You know, my hat is pitiful; Caleb, yours is a disgrace; Aaron, yours ain't too bad but I've saw better. We all needs us new hats."

"Man's a genius," snarled Ben. "*Course* we all needs new hats, boy. Problem is, where do we *git* 'em from?"

Bill's eyes narrowed. "I'm hatchin' a idee." He reflected for a half minute. "They's lots a civilians has good hats, right? We needs to git us some a them civilian hats."

Caleb said, "Stealin' pigs and chickens is one thing. But hats? That'd mean goin' in folks's homes. Huh-uh, not me. If I'm gonna git kilt I'd ruther be shot by Yankees than some Virginian over his *hat*."

"Don't have to go in nobody's *home* to git his hat, boy. They's other *ways* to do it." Bill's look was crafty, knowing, wise.

"Alright, you've got our attention, what's on yer mind?" cried Ben.

"Well, you know the train between Richmond and Petersburg has that long, slow grade that it has to slow down for? What if we could git folks to poke their heads outa the train windows so's we could knock their hats off?"

Caleb was incredulous. "Bill, that's the craziest idee I've ever heard of or you've ever thought of."

"What's so crazy about it?"

"Well, fer one thing, how're you gonna git folks to stick their heads out?"

"We'll make some kinda racket. We could fire our pieces. Let out the Rebel yell."

Caleb was not sold. "Alright, s'pose they do take the bait and poke their heads out. How're we gonna git their hats? Jist walk up and say, 'Would you kindly let me have yer hat'?"

"Boy, you gotta have some faith in ol' Bill. We'll have us some long poles to knock their hats off with."

They chewed on this idea for several seconds. Finally Aaron concluded, "I think it's got a chancet a workin'."

Ben was skeptical. "I'd have to see the place you're talkin' about, watch a train go by, see how slow she goes. *Then* I'll decide if it's got the chancet of a snowball in hell a workin'."

"You don't like to bet on no losers, do you boy? Alrightee, we'll jist go out and look 'er over. Caleb boy, you in this with us?"

"Sure. I wouldn't miss nothin' this crazy."

They got the sergeant's permission to be away from camp all afternoon with the promise of a new hat for him. It was an hour's hike to the railroad, and another half hour to the grade.

"What time's the train due, Bill?"

"Hell if I know."

Aaron could not believe his ears. "You mean you brought us out here and you don't know when or *if* a train'll come along?"

"Hell, it's wartime, boy. There'll be plenny a trains along. Jist don't git yer shit hot."

"Long as we're here why don't we go ahead and cut us some poles to poke hats off with," was Ben's suggestion. "How long do you figger a pole'll need to be?"

Caleb studied the terrain. "The trees is 'bout twelve, fifteen foot from the tracks. If we're hidin' ahint the trees and they sticks their heads out and we jump out we'll prob'ly need poles about eight, ten foot long."

Bill was ecstatic. "Boys, we been talkin' to Noah about the flood! Ol' Caleb here, wasn't he the one thought the idee was so crazy? Now who's showin' the most enthusiasm fer the project? I tell you, Caleb, you're a born criminal."

"Long as you got me all the way out here…"

They set to work finding limbs the right length, then pruning off excess side branches. They planned who would be where. "When you fire yer piece be sure you don't kill nobody," Caleb admonished them. When all possible eventualities had been accounted for they sat down and ate cold rations, washed down with canteen water.

Bill said, "The signal to start the racket will be me throwin' my kerchief out toward the track." Three-quarters of an hour passed, and then a train whistle was heard. "Git ready!"

Ben chirped, "Hey, if we don't git it did this first time we kin always try it better next un."

The train chugged up the steep grade and slowed to a crawl. They watched Bill for the signal. When the first passenger car was just beginning to reach him Bill tossed out his kerchief, then four muskets were fired accompanied by the Rebel yell. Within seconds several heads popped out of train windows and four poles began knocking hats off surprised and cursing heads. The train inched past them and soon disappeared over the hill. The jubilant conspirators collected seven hats and set off for camp.

Aaron cried, "I ain't had so much fun since my little brother got et up by the hawgs!" His cocked eyes were big as tomatoes.

Ben added, "I ain't had so much fun since my granny got her tit caught in the gate."

Chapter 18

▼

The Dallas **Spectator,** March 14, 1863

Typical of the treatment Southerners may expect if defeated and occupied by Yankees is that being meted out by "Beast" Butler in New Orleans. Butler suffered an ignominious defeat at Southern hands at Big Bethel Church in Virginia early in the war. Now as military governor of Louisiana, he has high-handedly decreed that any woman who by word or deed insults the Union flag, uniform, or army makes herself liable to be treated as "a woman of the town, plying her vocation". One woman who was said to have rejoiced volubly when the funeral procession of a dead Yankee soldier passed her house was arrested and sent to a heinous prison. The actions of the occupiers from Butler down to the lowliest private are those of contempt for the citizenry and the accepted conventions of polite society. So let us re-double our efforts to avoid this contemptuous fate!

* * *

As the spring brought its rebirth to Virginia, they were to move almost into North Carolina.

"What's up, Sarge?"

"The corps is bein' detached to go down to a place called Suffolk where the Yankees is threatenin' us. And they say they's lotsa food down there."

"Then let's go to where the food is at!"

It took them several days to march to their destination, days of increasing warmth when the rains didn't come. The farms were stirring with human and animal activity; they saw lots of newborn calves, colts, shoats, kids, lambs.

"Don't the sun feel good!" Caleb exulted.

"Reckon it'll take two months jist to git the chill outa my bones," Ben said.

Bill said, "Ben, I jist noticed that you walk like yer wadin' in water."

"That's 'cause I'm old."

Armies had neglected this part of the state, and meat and grain were plentiful. Most of the farmers were happy to see them until they paid for their purchases in Confederate money; then the farmers turned sullen. Some demanded gold but of course paper was what they were required to accept.

As they neared a river they came under heavy fire. "What in the hell kinda shootin' is that?" Bill asked the sergeant.

"Gunboats. 'Member back at our very first big action at Eltham's Landing, gunboats fired at us."

"Yeah, but I never seen one. Kin we sneak up and take a peek at 'em?"

They were ugly creatures, dark and trailing large clouds of smoke. "Reminds me of a raft with a milk bucket settin' on it and the whole thing on fire," mused Caleb.

They were put to work digging trenches and building forts for days, all the while under fire from snipers, artillery, and the gunboats. "Them Yankees sure is full a piss and vinegar," Ben cried. "Wouldn't you think they'd have a little more respect fer our attempts to git our work did?"

"I don't know which is worser, the Yankees a-shootin' at us, the diggin', or the rain," said Caleb.

"I do. It's the shootin'. Very few people has died from rain or diggin'," was Aaron's reply.

Ben retorted, "Ain't nobody likely to die from the kinda diggin' *you're* a-doin', boy. I'm a-thinkin' we oughta take a sightin' on you jist to be sure you're a-movin'."

Bill was silent for days, uncharacteristic for him. "Bill, you must be sick, 'cause you ain't runnin' yer mouth," Ben observed.

"I'm sick alright, sick a bein' shot at by them Yankee snipers ever damn day. They's a bunch of 'em over there in them weeds jist acrosst the river. I'm studyin' about swimmin' over there and settin' them weeds afire to spook them bastards outa there afore they kills me and maybe you boys too."

Ben laughed. "You're so fulla shit no wonder yer eyes is brown. First off, I don't think you ner nobody else kin swim over there, 'specially with Feds a-shootin' at you. Plus yer matches would be too wet to start a fire even if you lived that long."

Bill did not reply; instead he took his matches and placed them carefully on his head, then put his hat on tightly. Next he stripped off most of his clothing and slipped into the river. "Where in hell is he a-goin'?" the sergeant demanded.

"I think you jist answered yerself, Sarge. He's a-goin' to hell," replied Aaron, looking more wall-eyed than usual in his excitement.

"Well, don't jist stand there with yer fingers in yer butts, git yer pieces and give the boy a little cover fire!"

They shot as fast as they could, meanwhile monitoring Bill's progress across the river. It seemed an age before he crawled up on the far bank, and another before he was able to start a blaze. At first it seemed as if the rushes would not burn. "It's been rainin' too much, they're too wet." But at last they caught, and flared up surprisingly well. Bill dived in and swam furiously for home, his mates firing and cheering. He was helped ashore by Caleb and Ben, wearing the biggest grin any of them had ever seen on him. "You're a damn fool, Bill Tardy, you know that?" Ben exclaimed.

"And you're a hero, Bill." Caleb was beaming as much as Bill was.

"Hero, my ass. Jist didn't want them bastards to shoot us."

"They won't now, boy, you've drove 'em off," the sergeant said. "But that was a damn fool thing to do."

The next day General Hood sought Bill out. "Soldier, I've heard about your deed yesterday. Very brave. Say, aren't you the man who saved my life at Eltham's Landing last year? The one who disobeyed my orders not to load?"

"Yessir, General, I reckon I am."

Hood studied him. "Well, I think that if we had more brave men like you, this war would be won by us very soon." He shook Bill's hand and departed.

Caleb approached Bill. "Ain't you the one is always sayin' that officers don't know nothin'?"

"I'm the one. And he jist proved it."

*   *   *

Because of shelling and sniping they were forbidden to build fires at night and had to subsist on cold rations, mostly hardtack. One evening as they sat around in the dark gnawing on their supper the sergeant told them a story. "I jist heard today the craziest tale ever in my life. A day er two ago one a the officers said somethin' about one a the regiments not actin' brave enough in a engagement. Well, the officers in that outfit heard about it and one a them challenged the guy to a *duel*. Ain't that crazy? As if it ain't bad enough havin' Yankees tryin' to kill us, these damn fool officers is duelin' with one another."

"Sarge, do you mean they actual *fit* a duel?" Caleb asked.

"Damn sure did. Stood right up and fired at one another three times."

"Anybody git kilt?"

"Nope. One of 'em got a hole through his hat, t'other a little bitty nick on his neck."

"Sounds like awful pore shots," was Ben's observation.

"Sound like awful pore *thinkin'* to me. I been tellin' you boys these officers don't know shit from sassafras."

*   *   *

After a few weeks they were removed from their trenches and started back toward the main army. Before they left they bought up all the forage, grain and meat in the area. To the amazement of the commissary officers prices had risen remarkably since they had arrived. But the officers had the last laugh: not only were the supplies paid for in Confederate paper, they were hauled away in confiscated wagons by confiscated mules.

* * *

Again they marched through Richmond and were hailed as heroes. When they rejoined Lee's army they heard that in their absence a great victory had been won, but at a heavy cost. "Stonewall" Jackson had been killed, ironically and mistakenly by his own men.

"So we'll have to make do without that crazy old man," said Bill.

Caleb's reply was, "He may of been crazy but he was a hard fighter. And I wonder how many more has got to die before this war is over."

Chapter 19

The Dallas **Spectator,** May 19, 1863

The glorious victory of the Army of Northern Virginia at Chancellorsville over Hooker was sorely tempered by the loss of Stonewall Jackson, Lee's right arm and one of the Confederacy's hardest fighters. The fame of his "foot cavalry" is unsurpassed in Southern armies, even by the Texas Brigade, which incidentally was detached and did not share in the glory. Two ironies attach to the death of "Stonewall". First, he was mistakenly shot by his own men. Secondly, he survived the amputation of his left arm but died a few days later of pneumonia. His wife was with him when his soul departed this realm, which was on a Sunday, as he had always wished. Mrs. Jackson had brought their infant daughter, whom her father had never seen.

*   *   *

May 10, 1863
Dear Caleb,

    I was sorry to hear you were hurt but pleased that you are getting better. Mary must be a very good nurse.

    Bert Sammons is back home. I suppose you know that he lost his hand. He is feeling poorly about that and says what kind of a farmer can a man be with only one hand. Also his Paw is down in his back. Lucky for them that Quince is such a steddy hand.

    I have been over there a lot to try and cheer Bert up and also to see if I can help some. Also we have had Bert over here quite a bit, as it seems to make him feel better.

    Well take care of yourself Caleb, and give my best wishes to Mary.

Sincerely,
Elizabeth

    *   *   *

    Caleb scarcely knew what to make of this curt missive, so unlike Liz in its brevity and tone. But he had little time to ponder it because the Army of Northern Virginia had a Grand Review. The men got their pathetic uniforms and equipment in as good a shape as possible and paraded before the President, the Commanding General and his staff, and many Cabinet members and Congressmen and ladies. It took hours for all the elements of infantry, cavalry, and artillery to pass in review before the assembled dignitaries. Most of them liked parades, but not Bill. "I feel like a monkey in a cage, bein' ast to show off and strut my stuff in fronta all them stuffed shirts."

"Bill, you wouldn't be happy in a whorehouse with money stickin' outa ever pocket," Aaron cried.

"The hell I wouldn't."

*   *   *

When the long drum roll sounded for them to leave camp it was raining so hard that one could not see 20 yards. Before they had gone a mile they were soaked to their skins. It was ten in the evening before a halt was called, and they slept right on the ground just barely off the road, being too exhausted to eat their cold rations or to put up tents. Next morning they were roused and marched right back to the camp.

"Have I been a-tellin' you boys they don't know shit from sea water? Of all the stupid things we has ever did this has got to be the all-time champeen."

Caleb was inclined to agree. "It don't make much sense." At least they were allowed a day in camp to dry out and catch up on their rest.

Then they were marched out again, heading north. "Most any direction we go we're likely to see action, but you know damn well if we go north fur enough we'll git it fer sure," Ben allowed.

"Is that good er bad?" Aaron wanted to know.

"Good if we don't git kilt."

"Or if we win the war," Caleb added.

They crossed an old battlefield where the recent heavy rains had unearthed scores of shallow graves. The sight was gruesome: ruined equipment, dead trees, and shell holes dominated the view. Everywhere were arms, legs, even heads protruding from the soil as if to say don't forget we are here, don't forget our sacrifice. Most of the men were somber and feigned indifference to the presence of so many bones and body parts, but a few took a perverse pleasure in horrifying their mates with comments or even actions. Bill, for instance, seeing a hand sticking up out of the ground several inches, stooped over and shook hands with it, saying "Pleased to meet ya." The witnesses laughed a nervous laugh.

Next day the heat and humidity were both high, but the marching men were pushed along at a clip so demanding that even many of the hardened veterans fell out. It was with tremendous relief that they came to the Shenandoah River and waded it up to their armpits; after the hot march they were in no rush to complete the crossing of the cold stream. Then they camped on top of a mountain where the winds made it difficult to control their fires or for them to sleep. Some men caught colds.

Soon they were at the Potomac. "We been here before, last year. That's Maryland over there. That's where John the Baptist was kilt last fall," Caleb said reflectively.

The men were starting to undress in anticipation of another fording of a cold river. They waded across with clothing, muskets, ammunition boxes held aloft. On the far shore the band was serenading the brigade as it completed the crossing. There were others on the far shore: a group of Maryland ladies traveling in carriages past the half-or full-naked soldiers tried to get by as quickly as possible, accompanied by hoots and ribald remarks from the boisterous Texans. "Hey, ladies, like to see what a real man looks like?" "Hey, girlie, I like that hat, kin I have it?" "How 'bout a kiss fer a ol' Texas boy?"

*   *   *

If the people of Maryland loved them no more than they had a year earlier, in Pennsylvania they learned what real hostility was. But it was mostly a quiet hatred. Women would line fences or lean out windows as they marched past, peering at them as if they were British redcoats or Hessian mercenaries.

"I don't believe they're gonna invite us in fer supper," Caleb said.

A minor exception occurred when a little girl waving a United States flag cried as General Lee rode past, "Oh, I wish he was ours!"

As they passed through one village a woman asked, "What outfit are you?"

"Texas Brigade," several of them answered.

They heard a woman say to another, "They are the ones that has killed so many of our men."

"From now on maybe we oughtn't to tell them where we is from," Aaron offered.

"We could say we is from China, then maybe they'd say fer us to come on in and have some pie," Ben suggested.

"Has you boys noticed how fine the barns is up here in Pennsylvania?" Caleb asked. "And the haystacks seems bigger."

"And the roads. Some a the roads is hard. I ain't sure I kin walk on roads that ain't pure-dee mud," Aaron noted.

Bill spoke up. "They're called paved roads. These folks is richer than folks is where we come from. And they ain't had soldiers a-stealin' from 'em fer two years like them Virginians. At least they ain't yet, but I've got me a feelin' that's all a-fixin' to change."

Soon General Hood came riding by. "Hey, General, these folks looks awful fat and sassy to us. Do you reckon they ought to be lookin' this prosperous?" Bill quizzed him.

"Boys, you are in the enemy's country now. To me that means that you need to be alert to any unfriendly or hostile conduct by these civilians, and as far as their material goods, especially foodstuffs, I think you should do as you please." He was cheered by the ragged soldiers.

At the next farmhouse they were halted for a rest. Immediately men began to investigate the barn, root cellar, and outbuildings for things to "liberate". Bill knocked on the door of the house. A sour-looking woman answered. "What do you want?"

"We ain't gonna harm you ner nobody here, ma'am, but we are gonna go through yer house and look fer food."

"Oh no you ain't."

"Oh yes we is. Now lady, we kin do this the easy way where nobody gits hurt and nothin' much broke, or we kin do it the hard way, but we *is* a-gonna come in."

She stepped aside. "Jest don't take my china, it was my Grandmaw's. And don't take none of the pictures."

Bill led a delegation of Caleb, Ben, and Aaron into the house. When they emerged ten minutes later Caleb was laden with a brace of hams and three loaves of bread, Aaron had a large cheese and a plentiful supply of jams and jellies and apple butter, Ben was toting pickles and a side of beef and a dressed pullet probably meant to be supper, and Bill was encumbered with two large jugs of whiskey. They had a feast in the yard.

This scene was repeated in broad outline for the next several days. "We're gonna git so fat folks won't be able to see our eyes," Ben cried.

"Ain't it a good feelin' to feel yer belly crowdin' yer clothes fer a change, 'stead a havin' yer ribs pokin' out like a picket fence," Caleb said.

"I sure could git accustomed to livin' like this," said Aaron, his wall eyes bulging.

Bill was thoughtful. "You know the Yankees ain't gonna let us roam around eatin' up the countryside like this forever, so we best enjoy it while we can. There'll be a reckonin'."

One night Bill said, "I seen this farmhouse about a half mile off the road jist before we quit this evenin'. I'm thinkin' we ought to go take a look and see what it offers. Any takers?"

He and Aaron, Ben, and Caleb headed for the picket line, where they were challenged. "Where does you boys think you're a-goin'?"

Bill acted as spokesman. "Boys, us is a-goin' to do a little midnight requisitionin' at a rich-lookin' farm. We'll split whatever we git with y'all. Is it a deal?"

"No shootin', y'all hear? Alright, jist don't fergit to divvy with us on yer way back."

As they neared the farmhouse they could hear a musical instrument being played, none too skillfully, and female laughter issuing from the premises. They peeked in a window and saw three young ladies, one playing a piano-like instrument, one sewing, and one at the churn. They were speaking a language none of the Texans had heard before.

"Should we knock or jist barge in?" Aaron queried.

"Knock, a course. If we ain't invited in we oughtn't jist force our way in," was Caleb's reply.

They took off their shabby hats, slicked down their hair a bit with their own saliva, and knocked. After a pause the door was opened. All three girls were there, and their demeanor was guardedly, expectantly friendly. "Kin we come in, ladies?"

"Ya, kommen sie herein." They understood the words not at all, but the gestures were unmistakable.

The three young girls were all pudgy. They offered the Texans seats, then cake, then coffee. As the evening progressed it became obvious that the ladies would not be averse to some amorous pairing-off. One by one Ben, Aaron, and Bill drifted away to a bedroom with a hostess. Caleb contented himself with more cake and coffee and a perusal of the richly-furnished parlor. And thoughts of Liz. He remembered a hayride that the church gave, when it had suddenly begun to rain, and how he and Liz had burrowed under the hay to keep dry and warm, but it was the warmth of their entwined bodies that had been so sweet, until the chaperones had intervened.

An hour later they took their leave of the ladies. Three of them were grinning hideously. "Now what?"

"I think I seen a beehive over there a ways," Bill stated.

Aaron was hesitant. "Hey, I don't relish gittin' stung by no bees."

"Naw, they git all quiet at night. We got bees on our place, so I know what to do," Bill reassured him.

After sating themselves on honey, they located a milk-house, where they drank the cool milk to their hearts' content. "I'm so full I think I'll surely bust," cried Aaron as they started for their camp.

Ben said, "If you do, move away from me a little ways first 'cause I don't want you to bust all over me."

Caleb stopped suddenly. "Them pickets is gonna be mad at us 'cause we ain't bringin' 'em nothin' like we promised."

Bill had an answer for this quandary. "We'll jist have to sneak back in and miss them boys."

"What if we git shot?"

They didn't.

*   *   *

When the Texans entered the town of Chambersburg they received an early Christmas. Hood had already indicated that he regarded the enemy's worldly goods as fair game for his impoverished veterans, and in Chambersburg the men's search for a cornucopia reached full fruition. Dry goods stores, grocery, clothing stores were all hit hard by the soldiers, most of whom did not deign to pay for their "purchases". Caleb was embarrassed by his mates' greed, and when he selected a hat off a store shelf he pulled out his modest roll of Confederate money. The owner merely shook his head. "That ain't worth nothin' to me, you might as well jest steal the damn hat like the rest of yer thievin' friends." This nettled Caleb; fleetingly he considered replacing the hat, but in the end he walked out with it.

In the street Bill had a large clock, Aaron a quilt, and Ben two pairs of high-topped shoes. "Caleb, why don't you git somethin' fer Liz while you've got the chancet?" Bill said. "Hat er somethin'?"

"Naw, it'd jist git dirty carryin' it around."

As far as any of them could observe, none of the officers partook of the pillaging, but Sergeant Trammell had confiscated a mirror about two feet across. "Hey, Sarge, we'll be expectin' you to be extry purty from now on with that big lookin' glass to preen yerself in front of," cried Ben.

At the far end of town Caleb saw Henry Dowd laboring under a load of coats, shoes, and hats. "Ain't it awful hot to be a-carryin' all them coats, Henry?" Henry did not reply, instead sending Caleb a look of intense hatred.

They rested east of town, then were fallen in late in the day for a march that lasted all night. At each rest more and more of the loot taken in Chambersburg was abandoned.

"Bill, did you mean to leave that nice clock back there?" Caleb asked.

"I don't need to know what time it is anyhow. I have damn few appointments these days, you may of noticed. Besides, they's always somebody to tell me what to do and when to do it."

They could hear firing ahead and on the right. "Sounds like we're gonna git a little excitement," Aaron said expectantly.

"That's right, Aaron, you ain't been in no real *big* fights with us 'cause we ain't had none since '62 and you jist come up last winter," Caleb noted.

Aaron was curious. "What's it like? Is it skeery?"

"Naw, boy, it's a lotta fun," Bill kidded him.

"No, I'm serious. What's it *rilly* like?"

Bill said, "Confusin'. Noisy. And if it goes on very long, tirin' as hell. If we have to fight today, without no sleep last night, and it is a long battle, you'll be so tired tonight you'll be able to sleep propped agin' a tree."

They were formed into line of battle but were not ordered forward. Instead they came under intense artillery bombardment which lasted for hours.

"This is the part I cain't take," cried Caleb. "When we kin move around, even if it's straight into the Yankee fire, I kin handle it. But to jist set here and be shelled…"

They were ordered to dig in as best they could. "Wish I'd took a big shovel back there in town 'stead of a quilt. Quilt ain't gonna do me a lotta good now," Aaron said.

And it didn't. A shell hit right next to the stooped and digging Aaron, blowing him to pieces and showering Ben with blood and gore.

"Anybody else hurt?" the sergeant inquired as soon as he could reach the scene. Ben was shaken but miraculously uninjured, while Caleb and Bill were just stunned.

"Pore ol' Aaron. He ain't gonna find out what it's like," said a saddened Caleb.

"Oh he found out alright. The hard way," Bill said.

They were marched to a new location where they rested for an hour but without a chance to eat anything. Then they were moved yet again where they were crowded against a rail fence. Word came down the line that they should dismantle the fence, then begin to advance toward two little hills held by the Federals. The line of advance was mostly uphill, strewn with huge boulders, brushy, dotted with houses and trees, crossed by other rail fences and stone walls, with an intervening creek, and all the while a hail of Union artillery and small-arms fire was raking the path of their advance.

"I wish they'd give us somethin' *hard* to do," cried Bill. "Hell, we'll git plumb spoilt."

Captain Hamilton raised his sword and called to his men, "Forward, boys, let's show them what Texans can do!" He turned and faced toward the enemy, took two steps, and was hit by a minie ball which went in his left eye and blew out the back of his head.

As they advanced through the confusing terrain they became mingled with Georgians. The men did not know whom to take orders from, but since so many officers were going down there was lessening leadership all the while, so men just decided individually to keep going on toward the two little hills. Then word swept along the line that Hood had been badly wounded in the arm. "Let's win fer General Hood!" Caleb yelled, and others took up this cry.

It was very hot. Bullets were whistling and shells were exploding everywhere. Casualties were fearfully numerous, and the cries of wounded men were becoming more common, more persistent. Smoke was obscuring the battlefield. Caleb felt he had to pause to catch his breath and take a drink. He leaned his musket against a boulder and squatted, canteen lifted to his lips, when he saw a musket pointed at him. But it was not coming from the direction of the enemy, it was....Henry! Fifty feet away, Henry was drawing down on him. Caleb froze. Then he waved his arms. "No, Henry, it's me, Caleb! I ain't no Yankee!" Now he could see the hideous grin on Henry, and he realized that Henry knew exactly who he was and what he, Henry, was about to do.

Caleb jumped to one side and a ball hit at the approximate spot he had just vacated. Caleb got behind a boulder and a bullet thudded on the other side, sending up rock fragments. Caleb retrieved his own gun and took aim. Then he hesitated. "Do I really want to shoot Henry? If I don't he appears hell-bent on shootin' me." So he took aim and fired, hitting Henry in the chest. Henry went down like a felled tree, and Caleb hurried to him. "Why, Henry?"

Henry was in bad shape. "Cause you tole."

"But I never did, Henry. I tole you I never tole nobody."

Henry was coughing up blood. His face was ashen. "I don't believe you, Caleb. The way the boys was lookin' at me...." His voice was getting weaker.

"Henry, I'll try to find a stretcher-bearer for you." But Henry had stopped breathing, his eyes open in the stare of death. "Henry, I'm sorry I had to shoot you, but you didn't give me no choice." He wondered if Henry had heard his apology before his soul had made its departure from his body. He took Henry by the shoulders and shook him. "Damn you, why did you make me do it?"

Then the sergeant was standing beside him. "Come on, boy, there ain't nothin' you kin do fer him. Let's git on with our binness."

Caleb stood, took one final look at the prostrate Henry, and resumed his advance.

Ahead, Yankees were bunched behind a stone wall, firing. One of the twins from the next company went down, and his brother stopped to minister to him. Then he too was shot mortally. The Confederates mounted a charge that carried them over the wall, but they had no sooner won the position than an overwhelming Union counter-attack repulsed the out-numbered Southerners, who grudgingly retreated back across the ground they had bought so dearly in the last hours. Caleb was among the last to withdraw. He saw the captain with the real funny name, Barziza, go down, and there was no chance to rescue him. Then the Yankees picked him up. Caleb did not know if he was dead or alive.

Back at their jumping-off point the survivors fell exhausted to the ground, many of them sleeping through the night without stirring to eat or even urinate. Next morning while eating cold rations Caleb was joined by Ben and then Bill. He did not mention the incident with Henry.

Ben said, "Didja hear that General Hood was badly wounded in his arm?"

"Yes," Caleb replied. "Who has took his place?"

"Colonel Work."

"Ain't he the one whose daddy is the surgeon?"

"That's the one."

That day the main assault was made by Virginians on the Union center. The weary Texans were on a flank, behind a rail fence. Suddenly they came under attack by Northern cavalry. "I like this," cried Bill. "Us behind a fence shootin' at Yankee cavalry. A man could have a long, successful career as a soldier fightin' this way." No sooner had he completed his oration than a Yankee ball clipped his ear.

"Maybe you started celebratin' a mite early," Ben told him. But it was carnage: the Federals went down, men and horses, with frightful frequency. Caleb shot down a Union general. He thought, "As long as I been in this war I ain't real sure I've ever shot nobody, and in jist two days I've shot two fer certain. And one of *them* was on my side."

*   *   *

The wounded Army of Northern Virginia, defeated in the North for the second time in less than a year, retreated once more toward the Potomac. Heavy rains and high winds not only impeded their progress, but diminished their already sagging morale. "Boys, we ain't had no luck atall in the North," Caleb lamented.

"Oh, we've had plenty a luck. All bad," was Bill's reply.

The civilians watched them pass toward the South with an attitude vastly different from that when they had entered Pennsylvania. There was a look of smugness, of satisfaction, of "I told you so." But nobody said anything. They didn't have to; their demeanor said it all. So did the Southern demeanor: instead of jaunty and optimistic, they were downcast, spent, morose.

When at last they reached the Potomac it was swollen from the recent rains, so they had to wait in a sodden camp for three days before pontoons could be thrown across. It was not a leisurely wait. The army was on constant alert for an attack by the Yankees.

"Sarge, wonder how come they don't jump us?" Caleb inquired.

"I think we hurt them 'bout as much as they hurt us. They ain't in no shape to jump nobody."

Finally the river receded and they crossed to Virginia on the pontoon bridge. General Lee watched them as they filed by, mounted on Traveler. As the men shuffled by him, they doffed their hats, but they did not salute or cheer.

Chapter 20

The Dallas **Spectator,** July 11, 1863

This is the summer of our discontent.

First, our second invasion of the North was abruptly terminated at Gettysburg, Pennsylvania, when Pickett's division was repulsed with heavy losses. Then, to add to the South's misery, Vicksburg surrendered to Grant with many prisoners taken. One has to wonder at the loyalty of the Pennsylvanian Pemberton, and to question Mr. Davis's trust in him to command such a vital outpost. The Mississippi is now only tenuously held by our forces, with only a narrow crossing or two still open below Vicksburg.

*   *   *

Caleb was having trouble sleeping. Henry filled his dreams. Sometimes he would hold his fire and Henry would shoot him. Other times he would run away from Henry and no one would be shot. In one dream a Yankee shot Henry, in another Bill did, and once the Sarge did. Captain Hamilton was in a dream where he ordered Henry to drop his piece and shake hands with

Caleb, but Henry shot the captain through the head, and then Caleb woke up. In yet another version Captain Sealy and Henry both were aiming their guns at him, and he woke up screaming, rousing Bill and Ben and the new man, Rube.

"What's eatin' you, boy? You ain't hardly slept a good night since we got back to Virginia." Bill was more irritated than solicitous.

"It ain't nothin'."

"I ain't believin' that. Maybe you been at this war too long. Why don't you ast the Sarge fer a day er two off. We ain't that busy now nohow."

Sergeant Trammell *was* solicitous. "I been noticin' how you been actin' since we got back from the North, Caleb, and it ain't like you. Steada bein' easy to work with, you been all grouchy and not at all cooperative like usual. Anything you wanta tell ol' Sarge?"

Now was his chance to unburden himself of his load, but Caleb didn't. As much as he liked the sergeant, he wasn't sure his story would fall on sympathetic ears. Sarge was an old-timer, and he may not take kindly to the killing of a brother comrade in arms. Would he charge Caleb with murder? So Caleb kept his peace. "It ain't nothin', Sarge. But I could use a day er two away from camp. It'd give me a chancet to spend some a this money we got upon gittin' back from Pennsylvania."

He went into Richmond. The city had taken on a grimmer look since last he had been there. People were dressed shabbier, there were more wounded, the stores had sparser displays. He went into a bar but felt out of place. Caleb had never really cared for either the products served in bars or the types that frequented them. He wandered around the streets for hours and suddenly found himself in front of a church. He tried the door and went in. The church was cool and quiet, so he sat down and began to thumb through a hymnal. He recognized many of the songs although his church attendance had been sporadic and more for the social benefits than for the religious, and to be honest because Liz wanted him to go with her.

He had no idea how long he had been there when a middle-aged man with a broom came in through a door to the side of the pulpit and, unaware of Caleb's presence, began to sweep. Then he saw Caleb and, embarrassed, said, "I'm so sorry, son, I didn't see you back there. You go ahead with your devotion and I'll do this later."

"Oh no sir, I was jist about to leave. You go ahead on and do yer sweepin'." He rose to leave.

The man approached him. "I can sweep any time. Why don't you stay as long as you like? I'll come back. Unless you'd rather have somebody to talk to. I'm the minister here. My name is Gladson." He extended his hand.

"Caleb Walker, sir. Pleased to make yer acquaintance."

"Would you like to sit and talk with me for a while?"

"Yessir, I would."

They sat on the same pew. Mr. Gladson said, "I don't believe I've seen you in my congregation before."

"No sir, I ain't been in here before."

"Where are you from, son?"

"Texas, sir."

"Then you must be in the famous Texas Brigade. Didn't you boys just have a pretty hard fight up at Gettysburg?"

"If that's in Pennsylvania, yessir, we sure did."

"Did you lose any friends up there?"

Caleb clouded. "Well, we lost our captain. And Aaron from my outfit. And General Hood was hurt bad."

"Yes, I've read in the papers that his left arm was badly wounded, but it looks like it can be saved. Anybody else you know get hurt?"

Caleb wondered if the preacher could read minds. "Well, there was this feller got kilt, he wasn't a friend exactly…"

"Would you like to talk about it?"

Caleb began to cry, softly at first, then in great, racking sobs. He couldn't seem to control himself. The minister scooted over and embraced him like a child, but did not attempt to induce Caleb to stop crying. "You need to get it all out, boy. I'd guess you'd been needing to do that for a long time."

After five minutes Caleb began to be composed. "Who was the boy who got killed?"

"It was Henry." Then he relapsed into crying for another half minute.

"You said he wasn't exactly a friend. Then I have to wonder why his death upset you so."

"Cause I kilt him!" Caleb blurted out. To his surprise, hearing himself say the words was a relief, like once when he had had a huge boil on his leg and his Mother lanced it how much of a release it had been to get all that corruption out of his system. He searched the minister's face for a look of reproach or judgment, but he did not find it. So just to be sure he had been understood, he said, "I shot Henry Dowd, I kilt one of our own soldiers."

The preacher smiled ever so faintly. "Go on, son, you must have had a reason for doing what you did. Go on."

Caleb faltered, somewhat taken aback by this opportunity. He had expected condemnation or at least surprise, but what he was hearing was something bordering on acceptance. "He was a-fixin' to shoot me."

"Why was he going to shoot you?"

Then Caleb told the whole story, starting with meeting Henry back in Texas, the exaggerated attention, the incident in the creek, Henry moving to another tent, the killing of the rabbit, the threats, all of it. Then he related how at first he was sorry about Henry's death, but then how he had been mad at Henry for forcing him to shoot. Then he had been all mixed up between sadness, anger, and a nagging wonder if he might have contributed to the whole mess, or at least might have been able to alter the outcome if he had behaved differently. When he was done he felt tremendously unburdened, but he realized that the preacher's assessment still had to be endured.

"Son, it sounds to me like the boy was not right in his head. I don't believe you did anything to encourage the attentions he paid to you, which smack of those of a man who likes men instead of a man who likes women, if you follow me. Why he picked you out, we'll never know. But he sounds like a troubled man, maybe even an evil man." He reflected. "I have a strong feeling that God in His infinite wisdom understands your anguish and will forgive you for what you did. I only wonder if you will be able to forgive yourself."

Caleb pondered this for a minute. "Preacher, if you think God kin fergive me, I sure ought to be able to fergive myself."

"Now son, saying it is easier than doing it. You must realize that you are not perfect. You are just an ordinary mortal, subject to mistakes. God is a loving God. He loves us, not *because* of our weaknesses, but *despite* them. How many people do you know who are perfect?"

"Why, none atall, sir. I s'pose Liz, that's my girl back home, she comes as clost to it as any, but she's got her faults."

"Of course she has. We all do. But don't you love or at least like her despite the fact she's not perfect?"

"Yessir."

"And aren't there others you know that you like or love despite the fact they are not perfect?"

"Yessir."

"Then so does God love you and me and all others despite the imperfections we have. So He forgives you for shooting that boy in self-defense. Now you must forgive yourself."

"I'll try to, sir."

"If you ever need to come and talk to me again about this or any other matter, you know where to find me."

"Mr. Gladson, I cain't tell you what this talk has meant to me. I guess the Lord must of guided me into your church today. Good-bye, sir."

"Good-bye, my boy. And may God go with you and protect you."

* * *

Back at camp Bill and Ben noticed the change in Caleb right away. "Boy, from yer look I'd say you had some good drinkin' and maybe also a woman in

Richmond." Caleb smiled, and wondered how Bill could know him for so long and understand him so little.

Chapter 21

The Dallas **Spectator,** September 13, 1863

Now that the Confederacy has been effectively cut in two, disturbing reports are emanating from our neighbor Arkansas that there are those who are speaking of making a separate peace with the enemy. In view of the fact that the able General Kirby Smith has been put in charge of this western area, such talk borders on the treasonable. Our cause is far from hopeless. We must persevere, with our uplifted eyes on the ultimate goal of independence and the sustenance of our cherished way of life. And with God's help we will attain these goals. Our valiant forefathers endured Valley Forge and emerged victorious; so must we.

*   *   *

"Pack up, boys. The whole First Corps is bein' moved. The talk is that we will be away fer quite a spell." Sergeant Trammell was excited at the prospect of a change in scenery, and this feeling was conveyed to the men.

"Where do you reckon we're goin', Sarge?" queried Caleb.

"Don't rightly know fer sure, boy, but there is talk it may be Charleston, South Carolina. The Yankees is pressin' 'em mighty hard down there."

Bill stated, "I hear tell we're goin' to Tennessee to join up with Bragg. Or that Ol' Pete Longstreet may even take over from Bragg."

"May be. They don't tell ol' Sarge nothin'. Jist 'Git the boys ready and packed'."

Caleb needed only a few minutes to assemble his belongings and stuff them into his knapsack and the one hand bag. Bill was ready even quicker.

They marched south to Richmond, where the railroad station was a scene of wild confusion. At the platforms and in the yards was gathered the strangest profusion of rolling stock imaginable: box cars, flat cars, passenger cars, coal cars, mail cars, baggage cars. Onto and into these the troops were loaded. Caleb, Bill, Ben, and Rube found themselves atop a box car along with dozens of their fellows, with other dozens inside. As the trains departed they were ushered out of the depot by enthusiastic cheers from the citizenry, the women and girls waving handkerchiefs and the old men and boys doffing their hats and caps, some even throwing them into the air.

As the train moved southward, it being a warm early September day, the men below in the box car began to tear away the wooden sides of the car. "Hey, what are you crazy bastards doin' down there?" Bill wanted to know.

"It's too damn hot in here. Besides, we cain't see the country. And when we pass through these towns we cain't see the girls."

The train crawled slowly up hills, then picked up speed descending. The country through which they rolled was mostly wooded, punctuated here and there by cleared areas containing either cultivated fields or pastures, where the browsing cattle would raise their heads and gaze at them in their mild, bovine way.

In the numerous hamlets and towns the train passed through, knots of people small and large stared admiringly at them. There were yells of encouragement, smiles, waving. In one town, as the train slowed to a crawl, Bill pointed to one particularly attractive girl of perhaps seventeen. "I'd eat a yard a her shit jist to git a bite outa her ass," he grinned.

"If pore ol' John the Baptist could of heard you say that he would of fell off this train." But Caleb smiled broadly when he said it.

They changed trains. They were fed. They were not given a chance to clean up, and the cinders from the smoke-stack rendered them filthy. They were not allowed to lie down and sleep, but being soldiers they slept anyway.

At last they reached their destination, which turned out to be Atlanta. Here they left their excess baggage behind and started north toward Tennessee on one final train ride, led by "Aunt Polly" Robertson.

"I heard that General Hood is back over the division. Somebody told the sergeant they had actual saw him, with his arm still in a sling," Ben declared.

"I believe that 'bout all officers don't know shit from sugar. But as officers and generals goes, I guess Hood is as good as any." Coming from Bill this was a most generous compliment.

When the train pulled into the little station marked Ringgold, firing could be heard distinctly close by. They were hurried off the cars, marched in columns for a few hundred yards, then formed into line of battle. The advance lay through uneven country generously endowed with trees, shrubs, and vines which snared their legs. Confused and terrified deer ran from their concealment and charged in every direction. Hundreds of birds took flight. Federal artillery and small-arms fire were fairly light at first, but as the line kept moving forward and slightly downhill, the battle's tempo picked up. Men began to go down in increasing numbers. The officers became more persistent in their urgings. "Come on, boys, we've got them on the run! Don't let up, men! Keep moving! Keep firing! Let them hear the Rebel yell!"

The smoke was getting thicker. Caleb was sweating as he half-ran, half-walked on, stopping to re-load his piece. His mouth was dry, and he was pondering whether to stop and take a pull from his canteen when there was a flash to his left and a little forward. Dirt, rocks, and tree limbs showered him. For some reason he was on the ground. He tried to get up but he could not make his legs work. As he lay there trying to figure out what had happened, he began to feel a pain in his left thigh, as if a knife or pitch-fork had been stuck in it. Then he saw a red stain getting larger on his pants leg. "I been hit," he realized.

The stretcher bearers came at last and removed him to the rear. A surgeon looked at his wound. "I can't tell if the bone is shattered or not. We'll brace it and put you on the train and send you back to Atlanta where the doctors will be better able to treat you. As least you are better off than General Hood. He was badly wounded and has already had his leg cut off."

*   *   *

The hospital was hideously crowded, the cries and moans of the wounded heart-rending, the smell of sweat, blood, feces, urine, and medicine was overpowering. Among those tending the hurt soldiers were a number of ladies. Caleb remembered how Mary Tolbert had ministered to him back in Virginia. Women just seemed to be better at caring for sick and wounded folks. Oh, surgeons and doctors and litter bearers were alright and knew their jobs just fine. Maybe that was it: that it was just a job to them. But women seemed to do it because they wanted to. They were more, what was it, *tender*. Yes, that was it exactly, more tender, more gentle.

How he missed Liz!

*   *   *

"General Hood? They said it was alright if I visited you fer jist a minute. I don't know if you remember me, sir, but I've been in the Texas Brigade all along. It's Caleb, sir, Caleb Walker."

"Certainly, Caleb. Come in, come in. It's good to see you, soldier. I'm sorry I don't have a chair for you to sit on."

"That's fine, general, I ain't gonna stay but jist a minute, anyways. I jist wanted to check on how you was doin'."

"I'm coming along just fine, son. My leg is almost completely healed. Or I should say my stump."

"Yessir. I was awful sorry to hear you lost yer leg."

"It could have been worse, Caleb. I could have lost my life. And by the way, the boys of the old brigade took up a collection to buy me an artificial leg. Five thousand dollars." He stopped, his voice choked, tears in his eyes. When he was able to continue he said, "That is the most generous thing I have ever heard of in my life, in or out of the army. Why, I haven't even commanded the brigade since I was given the division over a year ago."

"Well, sir, I think it jist shows how much respect the boys has always had fer you. Even though you was only our commander fer about six months we have always called it Hood's Brigade no matter who was in charge."

Again tears formed in the general's sad eyes. After a few moments he composed himself. "I see you are on crutches, Caleb. Tell me about your wound."

"Well, sir, I must of got hit about the same time you did, only it was my left leg and your right. And yours was a lot worser, sir, because you lost yours."

"I am just grateful that you didn't have to lose yours, son. Are you getting a furlough to get rehabilitated?"

"Yessir, they said I could take off until the spring campaignin'."

"That's good. Where will you go?"

"Well, sir, I cain't go back to Texas because the Yankees has cut the Missippi. My Momma has some people over in Alabama and I have wrote to them and they say it's fine to come and stay with them a spell until I'm better. Then I will go back to the Army of Northern Virginia in the spring. I jist hope the brigade will be back there by then. I do like bein' under General Lee."

"Yes, Marse Robert is a great man. You know he was the superintendent when I was at West Point, and then I served under him in Texas with the Second Cavalry in the old army. A very fine gentleman. I just pray nothing happens to him. If there is one man who is indispensable to the Southern cause, it is General Lee."

"Sir, I best leave now. It sure was good to see you. Will you be leavin' the army?"

"Oh no. I can't leave the cause now. Others have continued on with worse wounds that I have received. And still others have given their lives, such as Sidney Johnston and 'Stonewall' Jackson. Just as soon as I can mount a horse I'll be back in there. Caleb, let me have your hand. Son, it is men like you who have been so loyal and have sustained our cause for so long, that I have the greatest confidence in our final victory. Good-bye, Caleb, and good luck."

"Good-bye to you, general, and may God bless you." He turned to leave but had an afterthought. "Oh, by the way, sir, I give a dollar on yer new leg."

Each had tears in his eyes as Caleb hobbled out on his crutches.

Chapter 22

The Dallas **Spectator,** October 3, 1863

From Atlanta comes word of another great victory, at Chickamauga, where Longstreet's detached corps, including the Texas Brigade, helped Bragg rout the Federals under Rosecrans. The only factor that saved the Union forces from total annihilation was the apostate Thomas. Otherwise the Northern rabble were sent precipitously back to Chattanooga.

Unfortunately Hood, who had previously lost the use of an arm at Gettysburg, had a leg amputated, testimony to his bravery in attaining proximity to the fighting. It remains to be seen if this gallant warrior will be able to return to action.

Also wounded was William Young, who recruited a company early in the war, and who had fought at Perryville and at Murphreesboro, where he was wounded. He was wounded a second time at Jackson, Mississippi in the Vicksburg campaign, where according to the official report he "seized the colors of his regiment in one of its most gallant charges and led it through."

Ector's Brigade saw action and suffered very heavy casualties. Terry's Texas Rangers were also an integral part of the victory. This signal victory in Georgia comes close to our great victory at Sabine Pass, where Lieutenant Dick Dowling and a literal handful of brave Texans turned back a force of thousands of Federals and their gunboats, further illustrating Southern bravery and Yankee ineptitude. The losing Union general was Nathaniel Banks, whom "Stonewall" made such a fool of in the Valley, Banks's command earning the dubious nickname "Jackson's Commissary".

*   *   *

The Hatchers had a small store and the post office at Pigeon Creek, Alabama. Lawrence had a wife, Helen, who was the sister of Caleb's Mother. Caleb had never seen his aunt and uncle, but had heard stories about them for years. Helen had written her sister in Texas four or five times a year, and had received a like amount of correspondence in return, with Caleb's and Jamie's assistance. When he was in the hospital in Atlanta Caleb wrote his Aunt Helen and apprised her of his condition. It was her idea that, if the wounded Caleb could get furlough, he would certainly be welcome at their place, Texas being not only so distant but also cut off. So to Pigeon Creek Caleb went.

"We've got plenty a room, God knows," said his effusive Aunt Helen. "Both our girls is married and both our boys has went into the army. Our oldest boy was killed at Gettysburg; the youngest is with the army around Atlanta. Just look at you! Why, you ain't nothin' but skin and bones. I'll vow I'll put some meat on your frame. Don't they feed you nothin' in that army?" She was corpulent and energetic, a slightly older version of his own Mother. "My oldest girl lives in Missippi and the youngest is in Arkansas. So just me and Lawrence is rattlin' around in this big two-story house. I think with your leg hurt you had best take a downstairs bedroom."

"Now Aunt Helen, I sure don't want to be no trouble to you and Uncle Lawrence. The leg is jist about healed up anyhow. I want to earn my keep while I'm here. If there's any work in the store or about the mail, let me take a crack at it."

"Boy, you listen to me. You're our guest here, and kin besides. And you been a-fightin' for us and got yourself hurt a-doin' it. If you think for one minute Helen Hatcher is gonna let you work like a nigger, you've got another think comin'."

But as the days and weeks passed Caleb was allowed to do more and more things around the store: stocking shelves, waiting on customers, sorting mail. He quickly became a favorite with all the ladies in the community. His slight limp and Texas accent gave him an aura of irresistible glamour.

But Caleb's thoughts were on one young lady only: Liz. He had not heard from her since the curt letter mentioning Bert Sammons. Did he have cause for jealousy? Bert had never struck him as a rival, but Bert was disabled and Bert was *there*. Did this make him alluring to Liz, as apparently his own disability had made him somehow attractive to the Alabama ladies?

*   *   *

Oct. 15, 1863
Dear Liz,

Well I am writting to you from Pigeon Creek Alabama. I dont know if you rember that my Momma has a sister hear name of Hatcher. Her and her husband runs a store and the post office. I am staying hear while my leg gits well. I got hurt up in Georgia and they said I could git away until spring and wasnt sure I could git home because the Yankees is suppose to be all along the Mississippi, and besides that is so far and this hear is closter. But I sure would like to see you Liz. I think about you ever day and speshuly ever night. This is a leter I hope you want show to nobody else even if you have showed them some of my other leters but not this one I hope. Liz, I am not sure that I have every tole you just how much I love you. Of all the girls I have ever saw you are the prettest, and the smartest, and all the things I like. We have always got along well togather and have not had no fights hardly atal (Maybe just a few littel ones but nothing serous) It just seems to me that me and you will probly git married when I git back. I dont know if this kind of talk supprises you, Liz, but it should not of. If you just stop and think about all the things we have said and did with one another, I think you will agree with me that I should be your husband and you should be my wife. No body else, no matter who, could ever be as good to you as I will.

Please write to me soon and let me know how you feel about all this.

Love,
Caleb

Chapter 23

The Dallas **Spectator,** October 10, 1863

One of the South's hardest fighters is Nathan Bedford Forrest. General Forrest has ranged with his cavalry through Kentucky, Tennessee, Mississippi, Alabama, and Georgia, consistently confounding and whipping Federal forces many times his number. He is a fitting tribute to Confederate cavalry who number also Jeb Stuart, Joe Wheeler, John Hunt Morgan, Texas' own John Wharton, Mathew Ector, John Whitfield, and Sul Ross. All these fine leaders do the South proud.

* * *

Liz had never been so tired. "There needs to be two of me," she thought, "one for our farm and one for the Sammons' place." The cotton was in on both farms, at last. She had done her usual stint on the Wright farm, having in the absence of brothers to do a man's work alongside her father. Then she spent as much time as possible helping Quince. With Mr. Sammons incapacitated with a bad back, Ben dead, and Bert with just one hand, a heavy responsibility had devolved upon the black man.

"Quince, I don't know how you can work so hard."

"Miss Liz, I could say de same 'bout you. Here you is a-workin' like a nigger over at your own Daddy's place, den a-comin' over here to hep ol' Quince on dis un. You sho is a strong woman, Miss Liz. And fer nothin' too."

"Hard work never hurt nobody, Quince. Besides, you ain't gittin' paid nothin' neither."

"No'm, I guesses I ain't. But dat's jest de way thangs is. I jest wish Mr. Bert didn't drink so much applejack. He might be able to be some *little* hep some kinda way if'n he could jest leave dat drinkin' be."

"I know. But you and me has got two good hands apiece, Quince. Poor Bert. It's hard for me to imagine bein' without a hand. I might take up drinkin' myself."

"Well, you has got a point dere, Miss Liz. Ol' Quince ought to be thankful he got two good hands, and not be a-jedgin' pore Mr. Bert."

Bert appeared from the house, a bit shakily. "Liz, let me walk you home."

"Fine. Good-bye, Quince."

"And a good evenin' to you, Miss Liz. Thankee fo' yo' hep."

The night was descending quickly as they negotiated the ruts leading away from the Sammons farm. "Liz, why do you spend so much time at our place?"

"Why, to help out. Your paw ain't in no shape to farm, and Quince, hard as he works, can't do all that needs doin' by hisself, and you…."

"And I am a damn worthless cripple, is that it?"

"I didn't say that, Bert."

"You didn't have to. As far as Quince is concerned, he's s'posed to work. That's what nigger slaves is for. He's got a place to sleep and he gits fed."

"Still, there ain't but so much a person can do, white or black. I just try to do a little somethin' ever now and again. If things was turned around and it was *us* in a fix, I expect you'd do the same for us."

"Liz, I don't believe a word a that. I think you come over so much 'cause you're sweet on Quince."

"Are you crazy? Why, Quince is a nigger. Now, as niggers goes, Quince is alright. He is respectful to me and he is a real hard worker. In fact, I don't think you appreciate him enough, what with all he does for you and your Paw. But as far as me bein' sweet on Quince, that applejack must be picklin' your brain, boy."

"Then if it ain't Quince yer sweet on, it must be me, 'cause I'm purty sure it ain't my ol' Daddy." With that he grabbed her with his good hand and his stump, intent upon kissing her.

"Now I *know* you've lost your mind, Bert. Turn loose a me before I knock your damn head off!" She thrust him away from her so violently that he fell.

"Goddamn it, Liz. You didn't have no call to do that. What was I s'posed to think? You come over all the time. You have me over to your place fer supper and Sunday dinner. I figgered you liked me."

"I do like you Bert, but not like that. I was just tryin' to do a little Christian charity toward you. And it ain't just you. It's your Paw. And Quince. I was just tryin' to ease everbody's load some."

"What you mean is, you was feelin' sorry fer me 'cause I'm a cripple. Well let me tell you one thing, Miss

Elizabeth Wright, I may of lost a hand, but I'm still a man. And I'm gonna show you I'm still a man." He began to try to unbutton his pants but the task was not easy with a hand missing.

"Bert, for God's sake, quit it! I know you're a man, you don't have to show me!"

His inept attempt to expose himself having failed, Bert began to whimper. "It ain't fair. Why did I have to be the one to come home crippled? Why couldn't I of jist got kilt like Ben did? It jist ain't fair." He was crying now.

Liz put a reassuring hand on his shoulder. "Bert, you're right, it ain't fair. But this is the way it is. You've just got to try and make the best of it. You've got your Paw to think of." She was patting his shoulder.

Again he made a grab for her. "Jist let me kiss you, Liz."

"No! Bert, I like you, but not like that."

"It's that damn nigger you like!"

"No it ain't, fool. It's Caleb, and it's always been Caleb. That's who I love, Caleb. I'm gonna forgive you for tonight, Bert, figgerin' it's the applejack makin' you act so crazy. But I'm tellin' you, boy, and don't you ever forget it, applejack or not, you better never try to lay your hands on me again, ever, you hear me?"

"You mean hand, don't you missy? I ain't got but one."

"I wish you wouldn't feel so sorry for yourself, Bert."

"Easy fer you to say. You got two good hands."

"Bert, we are talkin' around in circles now. I'm gonna bid you good-night."

She left him standing in the road.

*   *   *

Oct. 15, 1863
My dearest Caleb,
You dont have any idea how much I miss you. Do you realize it has been over 2 years since you left. But it seems like 20.

We have been working awful hard to get in our cotton crop. It is in and ginned up and we had a pretty good year. I have also been over at the Sammons place some helping Quince because Bert is not any help and Mr Sammons is still having truble with his back. Quince and me talks about you a lot and he says for me to say hello to you.

Bert has been drinking and really feeling sorry for himself. I dont like Bert very much.

It looks like Thomas Margarets husband wont be able to stay out of the army much longer. They are really pressing him and he is about to give up that he can stay out even if they do have 3 childern.

I have really neglected my sewing what with all the doings on 2 farms. Maybe this winter when the weather is too bad to be out I will get the chance to work on it again.

Boy, I sure hope your behaving yourself and rembering Liz. Write soon and offen.

All my love always,
Liz

Chapter 24

The Dallas **Spectator,** December 25, 1863

Another terrible loss! Chattanooga has been lost by Bragg. How a commanding general can allow his splendid army to be dislodged from such impregnable positions as Lookout Mountain and Missionary Ridge defies understanding. Mr. Davis needs to take a hard look at his friend Braxton Bragg, to determine if he is truly fit to command. Thus was the fine victory at Chickamauga simply thrown away.

One of the few bright spots in this disaster was the heroic fighting of a new brigade composed of four Texas infantry regiments—the 6th, 7th, 10th, and 15th; and four dismounted cavalry regiments—17th, 18th, 24th, and 25th. Its original commander, Brigadier General James Argyle Smith, was wounded at Missionary Ridge. Command then devolved upon Colonel Hiram Granbury, and the brigade soon voted to call itself Granbury's Brigade. Fighting as part of Cleburne's division, it fought a tenacious rearguard action that probably saved Bragg's entire army from destruction. For this action the division received the thanks of the Confederate Congress.

*   *   *

Caleb was gaining weight. Between his Aunt Helen and the other ladies in and around Pigeon Creek, he was being stuffed like the proverbial goose. He particularly liked her grits and cornbread. "Does everybody in our army look as porely as you do, boy?"

"Well, Aunt Helen, we don't always have a lot to eat, that's true enough. I s'pose they do as well as they can."

Every day he felt stronger. His leg was practically as good as new, which he attributed as much to the increasing amount of lifting and walking he was doing as to Aunt Helen's cooking and the passage of time.

"You ain't gonna overdo it, is you, Caleb?"

"No sir, Uncle Lawrence. Why, sometimes we walk 30 miles a day carryin' a full pack. Besides, hard work never hurt nobody."

The Christmas season was approaching. "Use to at Christmas we'd be a-doin' a lot more bidness, with folks a-buyin' fer their kin and also things to cook up fer their-selves. But with the war and all...." Uncle Lawrence's long sad face grew even more dejected. "Even the mail has slowed to near nothin'."

"Yessir. I sure cain't unnerstan why I ain't heard nothin' from Liz. I know the mail ain't completely cut off from Texas 'cause I keep seein' letters come through here from Texas." What he was thinking was, *Liz isn't writing to me because she and Bert have something going on.* He could not possibly know that Liz was not getting his letters either, thinking Mary Tolbert was the reason. What both of them did not know was that some Confederate mail was indeed crossing the Federal barrier of the Mississippi River, just not theirs. Such were the vagaries of luck and the Southern mail service.

*   *   *

Dec. 27, 1863
Dear Liz,

Well we had a prety big Christmas hear at Pigeon Creek considering the war and all. Aunt Helen cooked up a mess of chicken and black eyes pees and made a mince pie. I am giting so fat she had to let out my trowsers.

Its been prety cold hear. Some how I allways thought Alabama would be warmer sense it is call the deep south. Of corse I also never thought it could git so cold in Virginia niether, but sometimes I think Va. Is colder than the North Poll.

I sure do wish you would write to me Liz. If you are mad at me for any thing why dont you write it out and give me a chanct to say something back on my side. I must of wrote you four or 5 leters just sense I have been hear at Pigeon Creek. And sense the post office is right hear I would see it quick if you wrote me.

Well Liz, I hope you had you a good Christmas and so did all your peeple.

Love,
Caleb

*   *   *

Dec. 29, 1863
My dearest Caleb,

This has been our third Christmas a part from one another. If you had of told me we would be 3 Christmas's not togather I dont think I could of stood it. I pray ever night to God that you and me can be togather again and if we are I dont think I ever want to see your back disapeering over the horizon any more times.

Our Christmas was fine considering that lots of things is hard to get like suger. But as long as we have the farm we will always have plenny to eat. I give Maw a bonnet I sewed for her and also Rachel a littler one just like it. I give Paw a pome I wrote just for him.

I bet it is pretty cold up in Virginia. I rember you have told me the last 2 winters how cold it gets up there.

I sure do wish you could write me Boy! I know your busy but I fail to beleive your too busy to write to me, so do it!

All my love,
Liz

Chapter 25

The Dallas **Spectator,** February 22, 1864

A problem many feared has occurred. With the coming of war and the disposition of so many frontier units to the fighting fronts, Indian depredations have flared up. The murderous Comanches and their Kiowa allies have actually pushed the line of settlement back to the east, in some cases as much as 100 miles. This abandonment of farms and ranches to the savages has caused death and hardship to countless Texas families, and the end is not in sight. With our armies so hard pressed everywhere, no reasonable solution seems possible.

General Joe Johnston promises to be a better leader than Bragg; we wish the Army of Tennessee all the best.

*   *   *

It was late February and the Alabama weather was moderating. Caleb got into the habit of taking long walks along the country roads and through the undulating brushland leading to the creek. "I got to git used to walkin' again, and not jist on flat ground," he told himself.

Many Pigeon Creek young ladies were smitten with the quiet, modest Caleb, and none moreso than Martha Gantt. She was near Caleb's age and very flirtatious and forward. "Caleb, I see you takin' all those long walks; next time why don't I come along and we'll have us a picnic?"

He scarcely knew how to avoid it, so next day they did. They walked a mile or so until they reached an especially attractive spot where a large tree provided shade and a view of the creek's rapids. Caleb spread out the quilt and Martha laid out the fare.

"Caleb, how come you're so durn bashful?" Her freckles seemed to be dancing on her cheeks.

He was startled by her candor. "I, uh, don't hardly know what you mean."

"I *mean*, how come you don't hardly pay any attention to me when I come in the store? I've seen cigar store Indians that was more talkative than you."

"Well, uh, Martha, I jist ain't a big talker."

"Ha! That's like a panther sayin' he's not a big vegetarian. It's like pullin' teeth to get words out of you. Is it that you've never been around any girls before?"

"That ain't it. I got a little sister."

"Well whoop-de-doo! I'm talkin' about *big* girls, my age."

He blushed. "Sure. I got a girl back home in Texas."

"Uh-huh. And just what is her name?"

"Liz."

"Do you like her very much?"

"I sure do." His blush deepened.

"Have you ever kissed her?"

"A course." Now he was beginning to get indignant, both at her audacity and at the implication that he had never kissed *any* girl.

"Does she kiss good?"

"Martha, I wish we could change the subject."

"Oh, so it's getting too hot for you, huh? Well, I bet I can kiss as good as ol', what's her name?"

"Her *name* is Liz, and maybe you *can* kiss as good as she can, but me and you ain't gonna find out."

She was enjoying herself immensely. "Now who said I wanted to kiss you anyhow, *boy*. I've got plenty of *men* around here who would be only too glad to kiss me."

"Then I guess you need to git some a *them* out here on a picnic."

She giggled. "Caleb, you are a silly-billy. Can't you tell I'm just funnin' you."

He grinned sheepishly. "It's been a little while since I've been around any girls, I s'pose. I jist musta fergot how to act."

"You know what I think? I think that you would be bashful if you were around girls every day, girls by the score. And do you know what else I think? I think that you are so much in love with Liz that you won't ever look at any other girl, or woman, in a serious way as long as you live. I'd say that makes her a very lucky girl."

Then they had their picnic.

        *   *   *

He bade them good-bye. Aunt Helen cried, "Boy, you watch out for yourself, you hear me? I've done lost one boy in this war and I don't wanta lose another one."

Chapter 26

The Dallas **Spectator,** May 10, 1864

The Army of Northern Virginia has had another hard fight, this time near the old Chancellorsville battlefield. As usual, the Texas Brigade was in the thick of things. Meade, who took over the army of the Potomac just before Gettysburg, seems to be under the supervision of Grant, moved from the west a few weeks ago.

The latest attempt to invade Texas has resulted in a stinging reverse for Banks and his Federals, thanks to the efforts of General Richard Taylor, whose father Zachary obviously taught him well. Banks is one of the worst generals the North has, along with his fellow politician Ben Butler. As proof of our superior way of life we offer as amateur generals Bedford Forrest, Wade Hampton, John Gordon and Pat Cleburne.

*   *   *

Caleb was glad to be back in Virginia. When he rejoined his brigade the first person he looked up was

Bill, who looked none the worse. "You missed a helluva campaign in Tennessee," he said.

"I bet. But Alabama sure looked good."

"Got us a new general. Robertson is out, got crossways with Longstreet and sent back to Texas. Gregg is in; he was out in the West fightin' Grant. How is yer leg?"

"Bout good as ever. Did we lose anybody?"

"Ben got gut-shot and died about a week later. And Rube lit out. And the sergeant. You know, that was the funniest thing about Sarge. Well, not *funny* funny. Strange, I guess is a better way to put it. You remember how he used to always say, 'Boys, we are needed' when he fell us out? Well, you know how we used to rag him about maybe changin' to somethin' else? That day he said, 'Boys, we are *required*.' And then he went right out and got hit by artillry."

Caleb bit his lip and looked at the ground for a while. Losing the Sarge was a lot like losing his own father. The man had such good qualities: good at his job, patient, brave, funny, steady. Life in the outfit would never be the same with Sarge gone.

"We got us a new sergeant, name of Ridley. He is so tall he kin stand flat-footed and shit in a wagon bed." Caleb smiled. Bill continued, "You got here jist in time fer a big review. General Lee hisself is gonna be here to look us over."

As Generals Lee and Longstreet rode past the Texans a fervent cheer greeted them. Caleb thought that it was not possible for two human beings to look more grand than Marse Robert and Old Pete.

General Lee addressed them briefly, astride the great gray Traveler. "Men of the First Corps, the enemy is preparing to leave his winter camps and press us once again. All you gallant men have surpassed all that I and General Longstreet have asked of you. But now we are calling upon you yet again to rise to the challenge, to show the courage that has distinguished all your actions thus far. Let us join together to smite the invaders and drive them forever from our beloved soil!"

The cheer that followed was deafening. Lee had tears in his eyes as he raised his hat. Caleb said, "I would give my life fer that old man."

Bill replied, "You may git to."

"You know, Bill, when we was about to do our first fightin', way back there in '62, I was worried about bein' skeered. Turns out I wasn't that skeered. What I think about now is, odds."

"What do you mean, odds?"

"Well, don't it seem to you that we been awful lucky? Look how many boys has been kilt: John the Baptist, Tom, Wash, Aaron, Ben, the sergeant. How many times kin me and you keep goin' into a fight without the odds catchin' up on us?"

"Boy, I don't worry my head about shit like that. And think a this: me and you has both been hit, you twicet. Maybe that means we've done beat our odds."

* * *

The following afternoon they began moving into a dense, confused wood called the Wilderness, toward the sounds of combat. Most of the night they marched in columns along a plank road, the trees assuming weird shapes until finally obscured by fog. Near dawn they were allowed to rest and eat cold rations, but were admonished not to build fires.

Then they were roused and rushed forward. Word came down the line that the Federals were achieving a breaththrough and that they were urgently needed to stem what was in danger of becoming a Southern rout. As they hurried into a clearing, an agitated Robert E. Lee himself awaited them anxiously. "What brigade is this?"

"The Texas Brigade!" came the proud answer.

"I am glad to see it. You men of Texas have never let me down. When you go in there, I want you to give them the cold steel. *That* will stop the Federal advance!"

"We'll do it, General!" was the shouted reply.

Lee began to ride toward the front with the advancing infantry. Caleb said, "General Lee, you oughtn't go up there, it's too dangerous!"

Lee, eyes fixed toward the firing, glanced briefly at Caleb. "Son, I can't ask you to go where I am not willing to go."

Caleb began to cry. Except for the time in the church in Richmond, he could not recall having cried in the whole war, not when comrades had gone down, not when he himself was wounded. He grabbed Traveler's bridle. "General Lee, sir, I cain't let you go up there and git kilt. You are too important fer all of us." At this several other soldiers joined Caleb in seizing the horse and its rider. "General Lee to the rear!" they cried.

Finally Lee relented. "Alright, boys, I'll do as you request." And he turned the great gray horse and galloped to the rear.

The Texans now pushed on, bayonets fixed. But they saw no enemy. Only the strangely shaped trees were visible, now and then ensnaring sleeves and pants with their sharp limbs. The enemy's fire was taking its toll. And now a new horror was beginning: the woods were starting to catch fire. Soon the smoke was so dense that visibility was reduced to near nothing.

The advance slowed, stopped, and became a withdrawal. Wounded were left behind, their cries pitiful in the growing darkness. "Help me! Somebody please help me! The fire is about to git me! Please! In the name of God!" But to return to that arena of darkness and death would be futile, suicidal.

They returned to the clearing and formed up. "Where is Bill?" He did not return from the woods.

And then word swept over them that "Old Pete" Longstreet was dead, killed by his own men.

Chapter 27

The Dallas **Spectator,** May 17, 1864

Fortunately early reports that General Longstreet was killed in the Wilderness were false; he was only seriously wounded. It is not known how long he will be out of action. The South certainly cannot afford to lose another general officer of the caliber of "Old Pete", whom General Lee refers to as his "war horse".

In the West, Sherman appears ready to move on Atlanta, but he will have his hands full with Joe Johnston.

*   *   *

The next day Caleb had two nice surprises to help offset the loss of Bill: General Longstreet was not dead, only badly wounded ("That would have been too much, havin' Ol' Pete shot by his own boys on nearly the same spot where 'Stonewall' Jackson was kilt by his own men exactly a year before"); and the appearance in camp of Jamie.

"Well look at you, all growed up and filled out! You are a *man*!" They embraced warmly.

"You look awful skinny, Caleb. And you're *rilly* growed up. But I s'pose you've saw a awful lotta fightin'."

"More'n you know, Jamie. Fact is, I jist got back from Alabama. I was hurt in Georgia last fall and they let me go to stay with Aunt Helen and Uncle Lawrence. Actually they fattened me up like a hawg about to be butchered. You ought to have saw me before that. I was so skinny Aunt Helen said I looked like a skeleton she once seen in a travelin' medicine show."

"We didn't know you was hurt again or that you was in Alabama. The mail ain't gittin' through real reliable."

"What about Momma and Poppa and Annie and David?"

"They are fine and well. Everybody's been workin' hard. You wouldn't know Annie or David neither one, they are so growed up."

"What about Liz? You see much a her?"

"Naw, not much. She spends a awful lotta time over to the Sammons place."

"So she don't know I was hurt or in Alabama?"

"Not as I know of. By the way, I come up here with Thomas, her brother-in-law. We had a turrible time gittin' by the Yankees in order to git here, but we done it. He's got three young'uns and they still made him come. He ain't none too happy 'bout it. Me, I come because I wanted to."

"How is Poppa gonna make out with you up here, Jamie?"

"It'll be hard, that's fer dang sure. He's gonna try to hire Quince to help when times gits really busy."

"Quince is a good hand."

*   *   *

The tall, gangly Thomas was assigned to Bill's old place in Caleb's tent, but Jamie was put in a different company. "I don't want brothers that close together," proclaimed Sergeant Ridley. "They'll be payin' too much attention to each other and not enough to doin' their job." Caleb was disappointed with this arrangement but rationalized that at least they were close enough to see each other every few days or so.

Caleb pumped Thomas about Liz. "How does she look?"

"She's purty as a new calf, like always. Most near as purty as my Margaret. All them Wright girls is lookers."

"Was she spendin' a lotta time with Bert Sammons?" Caleb had never learned to be subtle.

"Well, you know I wasn't around their place a lot, our place bein' sevral miles away. But yeah, I think Liz was a-spendin' a lotta time at the Sammons' place, and seems like was Bert *was* over to the Wright's a right smart."

"Do you think anything serious was a-goin' on between Liz and Bert?"

"Now boy, I don't have no way a knowin' 'bout that. No idee atall."

"Do you know whether or not my letters to Liz was a-gittin' through?"

"Don't know about that neither, Caleb. Sorry I ain't no more hep than I'm a-bein'. But you got to unnerstand that I spend practical no time atall at their place. Got my own place and wife and three young uns."

"Sure, I unnerstand, Thomas. I'm sorry to be at you so strong with all these questions."

"Don't apologize, boy. If I was you and I'd been gone from my gal fer two and a half years and that gal was as purty and spunky as Liz is, I'd be a-astin' questions too. Say, how rough is this fightin' binness?"

"It ain't no day off, Thomas."

"How many in your outfit has been kilt?"

"Quite a few. In fact, I jist lost my friend Bill Tardy, he was with me ever since we left Texas together."

"That's too bad. Me, I ain't gonna git kilt. I got to git back home in one piece fer Margaret and my three little uns. And my farm."

"I hope so, Thomas."

*   *   *

Bill's death had been followed so quickly by the arrival of Jamie and Thomas that Caleb had not really had a chance to digest it. Only now was he starting to realize how much he had taken Bill for granted. Bill had always been there. True, he was not perfect. He had treated Caleb's relationship with Liz too off-handedly, as if it were only sexual. But you have to take your friends like you find them, warts and all. Bill was certainly dependable, and brave to a fault. He was almost always amusing. His irreverence for authority made for a nice balance to Caleb's almost slavish regard for orders and authority figures. Bill had been his best friend since Texas. Caleb had many dreams about Bill; in most of them Bill was not really dead. But in one especially horrible dream he had to watch Bill burn up, and he could do nothing to help. From that one he awoke crying and sweating.

*   *   *

"Boys, we got to beat the Yankees to the punch. They're tryin' to out-flank us. And if'n they do, Richmond is gone. So you're gonna be pushed 'bout as hard as you kin go." Sergeant Ridley was serious but not unreasonable.

The sense of urgency was felt throughout the demanding march and at its conclusion, where the men fell to digging in with every utensil at their disposal: picks, shovels, boards, knives, bayonets, even tin cups and spoons. No sooner had they settled behind their barely-adequate breastworks than the Federals assaulted them. The attack was repulsed with hideous Union losses, and a Rebel yell traveled the length of the Southern line.

"Hey, this is fun!" cried an exultant Thomas. Caleb held his peace. Then a second, more determined Yankee charge came at them. Despite the valor of the attackers, the grim defenders from behind their cover decimated the bluecoats, and the attack stalled, then recoiled. This time the cheer was more muted.

Thomas asked, "How many times kin they keep a-comin' at us, losin' as many as they are?"

"Oh, they got a lot more'n we do, Thomas. I s'pect they kin keep on a-comin' as long as they wants to. And we'll jist have to keep on a-killin' 'em."

"Seems like a awful helluva waste a good men to me."

"War is like that," was Caleb's judgment.

Many of the men scrambled out from behind the earthworks to retrieve the Enfield rifled muskets of the slaughtered Yankees. "Ain't you gonna git one, Caleb?"

"Naw, I like my Springfield better."

Now came a third Federal charge, heavier than the previous two. Slowed though they were by having to climb over the bodies of their mates, the determined attackers were making dents in the Confederate lines. Here and there a man scaled the breastworks only to be shot or bayoneted by a defender. Caleb saw Thomas freeze when a Union corporal loomed over him, carbine pointed at Thomas' breastbone. Caleb drove his bayonet into the corporal's lower abdomen and then retrieved it just in time to avoid being fallen upon. The man knocked Thomas down, but he bounced up and resumed his place in line. Caleb thought, ol' Thomas is gittin' broke in real fast, and he ain't doin' a bad job a catchin' hold.

The Northern commanders changed tactics. They stopped charging and had their dug-in troops open up a medium-range fire by sharpshooters and snipers, hoping that their greater numbers could inflict more casualties by attrition than they would have to take. But the Texans held their own at this game. They kept their heads down most of the time, and when they did deign to fire it was usually with deadly effect.

A night and a day and another night passed in this stalemate. By now the heat and the passage of time had bloated the Yankee corpses in front of the earthworks, and the stench of rotting flesh was becoming untenable. Many of the Southerners tied kerchiefs over their noses, but the pervasive smell could not be easily blocked out. Vomiting was common. Finally an officer had a solution: barrels of tar were brought from the rear, laboriously rolled in front of the entrenchments and set afire.

Although the burning tar was acrid and objectionable, it was preferable to the smell it helped cover.

"Why don't the Yankees come and git their dead and bury 'em?" Thomas inquired. "Ain't they sich a thing as a truce fer that?"

"Sometimes they do. Jist depends on how pig-headed both sides is," Caleb informed him.

"Looks to me like our people would welcome it was the Yankees to take away them pore stinkin' boys."

"Thomas, one thing you'll learn awful quick is, the most logical and smart thing to be did seldom is what *is* did. And I'm a-talkin' 'bout both sides."

The men took turns sleeping and eating during this time. Total relaxation was out of the question since a renewed attack could come at any moment, night or day.

Then they were aware that the enemy in front of them had gone, so they too were marched away. It felt good to stretch out after so many long hours crouched behind their breastworks, but the march lasted seemingly forever. In 20 hours they were fallen out to rest for only two one-hour breaks.

"My feet is sure hurtin'. Ain't yours?" Thomas pleaded.

"You'll git used to it."

They dug in again, and again they had to withstand a Yankee charge, and again they sentenced a frightful number of attackers to death. They had been ordered to wait until the bluecoats were within 20 yards of their works, and the volley fire was pure carnage. This time there was no second assault. The sun was unmercifully hot, and by the third day the ripened victims of the slaughter were horrible to behold and to smell.

Thomas cried, "I ain't been in this here war hardly no time atall, yet I've figgered out the Yankee strategy to whup us. It's to stink us out."

Finally the Yankees asked for a truce to bury their copious dead, and it was granted. "Thank God!" was on the lips of every Texan who had endured the stench that he had helped create.

The Northern litter bearers, kerchiefs tied over noses and mouths like stagecoach robbers, came hour after hour removing the pitiful remains of their comrades. Then the bands behind both lines struck up, playing many of the old favorites. When the Federal band played "Yankee Doodle Dandy" and "The Battle Hymn of the Republic" the Northern soldiers cheered; the Southerners tried their mightiest to drown out the music and the cheers with boos and hisses. The converse happened when the Rebel band played "Dixie" and "The Bonny Blue Flag". Unbelievably, some newspapers were even exchanged during the truce period. Then suddenly the cease-fire was over and men began again to try to end each other's lives.

"Seems like a strange way to run a war," observed Thomas.

*   *   *

"How you been, little brother? What was it like, bein' in yer first fights?"

The color rose in Jamie's cheeks. "It was differnt. I've thought a bunch about how it'd be to be in a battle, and some of it was about what I expected. What supprised me was the noise, the smoke, and how thirsty I got."

"What about the smell?"

Jamie grimaced. "That part is pitiful. I've smelt dead animals before, a course. 'Member that time me and you found that cow a ours that had been dead about a week and how awful it was? 'Specially since we had to bury it. But God in heaven, this was 'bout a hunderd times worser. Them pore boys, all blowed apart and swole up and...." His voice trailed off and he shook his head in genuine remorse.

"Course it's them er us. Was you skeered?"

"Didn't really have no time to be. Too busy loadin' and firin'...."

"Made any friends yet?"

Jamie smiled. "Yeah. This guy Michael O'Grady, Irish boy. Jist come over to Galveston 'bout a year before the war. Me and him is purty good friends. He's Catholic. I never seen a Catholic before, 'cept a Meskin."

"Naw, I never either. Is he a good fighter?"

"Real good. Says he jist pertends the Yankees is English and that keeps him a good mad on."

"How is yer feet holdin' out?"

"They hurt purty fierce. That last march nearly done 'em in."

Caleb was enjoying playing the twin roles of solicitous big brother and seasoned veteran. "How 'bout food? You gittin' enough to eat?"

"Well, you know I ain't much of a eater anyhow. But yeah, I'm doin' alright. Ain't much variety, are it? Bacon and corn meal, then corn meal and bacon." He laughed restrainedly at his own little joke. "How did Thomas do?"

"He done good."

*   *   *

Again the enemy abandoned the ground in front of them. They were force-marched south and went into trenches already prepared. "Now that was awful nice a somebody to dig these ditches fer us," Thomas cried. "Wonder who done it? Other soldiers?"

"Prob'ly slaves."

"Wonder if we gits short-handed enough if'n they'll use slaves as soldiers?"

Caleb thought about this for a minute. "Don't seem sensible to me that a slave'd be a good soldier."

"Why not, Caleb?"

"Well, don'tcha see, if our side wins that means he'll stay a slave. If'n I was a slave I don't think I could bring much enthusiasm to fightin' fer our side."

"Yeah, I see what you mean. Then how come slaves digs these ditches fer us and sich like?"

"I don't see that they have no choice about it, no more'n they has a choice 'bout nothin' else they has got to do. That's what bein' a slave means. You do what the master tells you."

"Then why cain't they be give guns and told to fight fer our side?"

Caleb smiled. "A man with a gun in his hands might feel he's got some say comin' 'bout what he do and don't do, whereas a man with only a shovel or a pick ain't as likely to speak up too smart to a man holdin' a gun on 'im and sayin' to dig a ditch here."

Thomas chuckled. "You got a point there, boy."

Now sniper fire from the Yankees began and gradually intensified. Texans who were not careful to keep their heads down were hit, some fatally. Caleb worried about Jamie. After an hour or so of this deadly irritation the mood of the boys in gray changed from sullen to angry, and they spontaneously charged the enemy with a Rebel yell. The startled Federals relinquished their position and fled in disarray. The Southern cheer was loud and joyous.

"Man, we sure whupped them Yankees, didn't we Caleb?"

"More supprised 'em than whupped 'em. They didn't think we'd charge 'em from outa our ditches. Supprised *me*."

*   *   *

They were put on a train to Petersburg. Upon leaving the cars they were offered coffee by the citizens of the town. "We sure 'preciate you Texas boys bein' here."

"We 'preciate the coffee," said a grinning Caleb. "We don't git much coffee. Git a lotta substitutes but very little real coffee. And you folks is got it by the hogsheads."

"And we're proud to share it with you."

Caleb had a chance to visit with Jamie for a few minutes, then they were parted and entered trenches. These were the most elaborate and carefully prepared they had ever seen: seven feet deep with firing platforms. As they settled into their new surroundings the Federals began a constant mortar fire that was especially demoralizing in that even if a man kept his head down and was thus immune to being shot by a sharpshooter, he could still be killed or wounded by the terribly impersonal mortar fire which, coming in as it did from above, was no respecter of cover.

"I've always hated mortar and artillry fire more'n anything," stated a grim Caleb. "Don't do no good to be in no trench. If it's meant fer you it'll git you."

"And ain't it hot? Caleb, why don't we put a blanket up to keep out the sun, and hold it in place with a couple a planks." They did, but the flow of air was restricted, so they took off their shirts. One effect of this was to give the flies, gnats, and mosquitoes more skin to torment.

"What would you give fer a good bath right now, Caleb?"

"I could sacrifice 'bout a year away from this here hotel."

They were losing an average of a man a day to the enemy snipers. These unfortunates had to be buried in shallow graves right behind their entrenchments, so that when it rained the grisly corpses were soon exposed, followed all too soon by the peculiar putrid-sweet odor of decomposing human flesh, and a million flies.

Every day was like the one before, and the one before that. When it rained the bottom of the trench became a slimy, sodden mire. And when it didn't rain the dust choked them. To relieve the tedium men would put their hats on sticks and hoist them to test the marksmanship of the Yankee snipers. The monotonous food—corn meal bread, bacon, cow peas, rice—became more scarce and finally was distributed every other day.

"I am goin' to write a thank-you letter to the commissary." Thomas had a twinkle in his eye.

"How come?"

"Cause the food is so bad, I'm a-gonna say thank you fer a-cuttin' it back."

"Thomas, you're a caution."

"Caleb, do you s'pose them fellers at the commissary eats as porely as we does? I jist wonder if maybe they don't take a extry portion fer theirselves."

"That has crossed my mind. I don't think they'd be hardly human if'n they didn't pinch off a little somethin' extry."

"I am so hungry I could eat the ass out of a buzzard. You know, Caleb, when I git home I'm gonna plant less land in cotton and more in food crops. I don't never wanta be hungry agin. I'm gonna have the damdest biggest garden in Texas. Corn. Tomatoes. Potatoes. Cucumbers. Onions. Beans. Peas. Watermelons."

"Hush up, Thomas, you're makin' my mouth water somethin' fierce. I kin recollect when we first left Dallas way back in '61, we actual throwed food away 'cause we cooked too much of it. What I wouldn't give right now fer some a that bacon we jist pitched right on the ground. That were good fresh bacon, not like this sorry stuff we're a-gittin' now."

* * *

"Sergeant Ridley, I think I hear diggin' under us."

"You do, boy," he replied to Caleb. "The Yankees is a-tunnelin' under our works."

"Wonder why?"

The sergeant looked perplexed. "Beats the hell outa me. Maybe they thinks they kin dig a hole right under us and come up at Petersburg. Or even Richmond."

To monitor the progress of the surreptitious excavating, Thomas would drive a stake in the bottom of the trench and bite on it. "Whatever are you a-doin', boy?" an incredulous Sergeant Ridley wanted to know.

"I kin feel them a-diggin' through my teeth." This earned Thomas the nickname Peg-Biter from the sergeant, which soon was shortened to Peg.

On about the hottest day of their duty in the trenches, after six weeks in this purgatory, just when they were all convinced they would suffocate under the sun-blocking blankets and tarpaulins, the Texans were relieved by South Carolinians and sent to a quiet sector near Petersburg, where they remained for a lovely week. After all that time spent with the threat of death facing any man who raised his head too high, many found it hard not to walk with a stoop. But not Caleb. "When you're short like I am you don't have to fret quite so much as you tall boys does."

They found walking erect and running and bathing afforded them heretofore unappreciated joy. "You know, a man don't 'preciate the little things enough. We takes way too much fer granted," was Thomas's analysis. "Maybe we was did a favor, havin' to stoop around in all that muddy shit."

"Why Peg, you're a regular philosopher," Sergeant Ridley pronounced.

*   *   *

Caleb and Thomas went into Petersburg. The small town was doing a lively business in gambling, bars, and prostitution—any services that catered to off-duty soldiers. Most of the town's "decent" young women had been sent away to stay with relatives in Richmond or better still points west, away from the siege, the besiegers, and especially the besieged.

Caleb said, "Thomas, you ain't tole me yet about when you got signed up to come into the army."

"Well, they jist come out to my place and said I had to go in. I said, 'But I got a wife and three young'uns.' And they said, 'So has a bunch of other fellers, but we is short-handed. You got to go in, boy.'

"So I reported in Dallas, and this officer-like feller, he ast us if'n we druther be in the artillry, or the cavalry, or the infantry. We ast what was the differnce, and he says, 'Well, the artillery is them big guns;' so I says, 'That ain't fer me, my ears is too tender'. So he says, 'Well, that leaves the cavalry or the infantry'. So I says, 'What is the differnce in them two', and he says, 'In the cavalry you gits to ride a horse'. So I says, 'Hold 'er right there, I'll take that there infantry, 'cause if they tells us to retreat, I don't want no *horse* a-slowin' me *down*'."

Caleb had good laugh. "Thomas, you're a pure-dee caution."

The two Texans walked around for an hour, poking their heads into stores now and then, had one beer apiece, and returned to camp. They told Sergeant Ridley about their day. "You boys is gonna have to cut down on all that wild livin'. By the way, did y'all hear about the big explosion?"

"Naw, what happened?"

"Well, you 'member that diggin' we heard in them trenches? Them Yankees musta been puttin' explosives under there 'cause they blowed it up and it made the biggest hole you've ever saw. Kilt a bunch a them South Carolina boys. Right where we was at. Think of it!"

"Then what happened?"

"Well, they tried to send their soldiers through, but they was kindly down in this here hole, don't you see, so our boys jist shot 'em like shootin' fish in a barrel. I heard tell a awful lot of 'em was nigger soldiers."

" So the idee was, not to dig by us, but to blow a gap in our ditches so's they could pour through."

"I knowed you'd unnerstand it, Caleb. What about you, Peg, you got it figgered out too?"

"I got the picture, Sarge," smiled Thomas. "I guess the Lord must surely be a Texan."

"It don't look like he's from South Carolina," Caleb noted.

The sergeant added, "Or a Yankee."

*   *   *

While in the restful camp Caleb wrote Liz:

July 25, 1864
Dear Liz,

I don't have no idee atal if you will git this, sense I have not herd from you in so very long. Over a year in fack. Just in case you do git this I will catch you up on what I been doing. We was in Pencilvania about a year ago then we was in Georgia and I got hurt in the leg their and went to see my aunt Helen and her husband in Alabama. Now I am back in Virginia. Jamie and your brother in law Thomas is both hear with me in fact Thomas and me is right togather but Jamie he is in another company. We been fighting prety hard and we been in ditches a lot to keep the Yankees out of

Richmond. A lot of my frends has been kilt but I am fine, my best frend Bill Tardy he was kilt and I miss him a awfull lot. I hope you are fine Liz I sure do miss you a lot and also I love you. I didn't have no idee how much I love you untill I got way off up hear so far from my sweet Liz. Do you know we have not saw one another for neerly three year.

I know you must be working awfull hard on your place. I cant wate to git back home and be a farmer agin and not have to be a soljer no more.

I know the Yankees has cut the Mississippi and you may not git this but if you do tell ever boddy I say hello and write to me if my leter got to you then may be your's will git to me.

All my love for ever

Caleb

P.S. We are in camp now and out of danger. Me and Thomas went to town, Petersburg the other day. I seen a bonet in a store I would have bougt it for you but I don't know how I would git it to you.

Chapter 28

The Dallas **Spectator,** July 29, 1864

The best of news! The gallant John Bell Hood has been given command of the Army of Tennessee defending Atlanta from Sherman. Not that Joe Johnston was doing so badly, but his forte is defense, and the bold Hood thinks only of the attack. Ector's Brigade is assisting in the defense of Atlanta, and will undoubtedly acquit themselves well when Hood goes on the offensive.

In the East, Lee is doing a masterful job parrying Grant's thrust toward Richmond, with the Texas Brigade performing its usual yeoman work.

General Forrest has again proven his genius by decisively whipping a much larger Federal force at Brice's Crossroads in Mississippi.

*   *   *

The restful, safe week in camp accelerated to its inevitable end, and the brigade was ordered back into the trenches. "I'd ruther be beat with a cuckleburr stick than git back in there," cried Thomas. "Does we have to,

Sarge? Cain't we put the commissary or maybe the quartermaster boys in there 'stead a us? 'Pears to me like they're missin' the best part a the war. What kinda stories is they gonna have fer their grandchildern? 'I handed out underwear durin' the war' or 'I give out beans'. Now I ask you, is that any kinda way to treat them boys in the rear area? Sarge, I'll bet you that if we jist ast them fellers to volunteer they'll take our places in a snap."

"Peg, if we was in a talkin' war with the Yankees I'd nominate you to replace General Lee." The sergeant's feigned impatience was transparent.

But after one day in the trenches they were withdrawn. "What does you make a that, Caleb?" Thomas queried as they were marched out and headed north.

"If ol' Bill was alive he'd have somethin' funny to say 'bout how them officers don't know nothin'. Me, I ain't gonna be critical of no decision that gits me outa that hell-hole."

They crossed the James River and took up a position outside a fort. "What's the name a that outfit, Sarge?" asked Caleb.

"Fort Harrison. There ain't hardly nobody in it, mostly artillry. What we is supposed to do is keep the Yankees out of it. We're gonna build us some breastworks startin' right after we cooks us some vittles."

This part of the front remained quiet for several weeks. They kept hearing stories about the fighting further south, around Petersburg. "Ain't you glad we ain't down there no more?" Thomas asked.

"Oh, I 'spect we'll git our turn soon enough," Caleb answered.

About a hundred yards from their works was an apple orchard which the Texans visited from time to time to vary their diet. Early one morning when the orchard and the Texan lines were cased in a dense ground fog, a Union attack erupted from the orchard. The alert Texans were quickly at their places, pouring a murderous fire into their assailants. "I believe them soldiers is niggers!" The black brigade, led by white officers, made a determined charge at the Rebel lines, but they were enfiladed by their foes and were mowed down. The survivors retreated, those who were not captured. The fray had lasted five minutes, costing the Federals 194 black soldiers and 23 of their white officers killed. Forty-three black prisoners, fear written large on their faces, were at the mercy of the Texans.

Although the Texans had not lost a man in the fight, there was intense sentiment for killing all the prisoners. They were incensed that these men, whom they had always regarded as inferiors, would presume to fight against them as equals. Caleb jumped to their defense. "Cain't you boys see that these fellers was brave? We wouldn't shoot no white prisoners, would we? Then why would we want to shoot colored? It ain't their fault they're black. Besides, the Yankees is a-usin' them. They're like victims. We oughtn't be mad at them fer a-fightin' agin us. They was jist a-doin' what they been tole like we does. If you want to kill somebody, kill the ones as sent 'em agin us."

This speech, so surprising coming from the usually quiet Caleb, saved their lives. Although they grumbled, the Texans saw the wisdom of Caleb's reasoning, and their mood quickly cooled. Most of the blacks, faced with the prospect of Southern prison camp, volunteered to be orderlies for the Texans, which further mollified them, accustomed as they were to blacks being in a subservient role.

Caleb thought of Quince, practically his only contact with a member of the subject race. He only hoped that in a similar circumstance someone would speak up to save a man as admirable as Quince.

*   *   *

But Quince was not thinking about Caleb. He had other, more pressing concerns.

Chapter 29

▼

The Dallas **Spectator,** September 17, 1864

Atlanta has been lost, which is terribly unfortunate, but General Hood, now free from the responsibility of defending Atlanta, can now do what he has always done best: attack. The Union army under Sherman will soon feel the wrath of the Army of Tennessee.

The war in the East has become one of attrition, but Lee, among the best in history on the offensive, is showing Grant something about defense. Remember that General Lee's training was in engineering, so no one is better disposed to use entrenchments.

*   *   *

Quince didn't know what Mr. Bert was thinking about. He certainly hadn't been raised that way. His Daddy was a God-fearing man who knew right from wrong and had tried to teach his two boys the difference. And Mr. Bert's Mother was a very fine Christian lady until her untimely death from a mysterious fever.

Yes, Mr. Bert knew better. Was it the fact that he had lost a hand in the war? Or maybe it was the loss of his brother Ben. Quince hated to sit in judgment of any man, especially a white man. Miss Liz had talked like neither she nor Quince himself should judge Mr. Bert. But stealing? From his neighbors, many of whom had been so generous to him and his Daddy? It seemed shameful.

At first Quince had tried to ignore the signs. The extra chickens in the pen. Then a new shoat. Then a new calf. But now Mr. Bert seemed to be concentrating on liquor. He was drunk more often, and there was no way he could afford to buy all the liquor he was consuming. Quince briefly thought about talking to Mr. Sammons, but decided the old gentleman had enough troubles with a bad back that kept him in bed almost constantly now, a son killed in the army, and a hard-drinking one-handed son that the old feller didn't need to know was a thief. So Quince held his tongue.

The only person he felt he might be able to discuss Mr. Bert's stealing with was Miss Liz. She was level-headed and would probably know what to do. He brooded over this for weeks, and finally one day he sprang it on her.

"Miss Liz, I think Mr. Bert is a-stealin' from folks 'roun' here."

"Are you sure, Quince? That's a mighty serious accusation."

"Yessum, I knows it is. But look at dat dere shoat. We ain't had no shoat looks like dat. An' see dat calf, with de white spot on its right side? Dat's new. I knows I ain't stole it an' Mr. Sammons he ain't been fit to go nowheres to git it."

"Could Bert have bought 'em?"

"No'm. He ain't got no money to buy no calf ner no shoat. An' extry chickens been 'pearin', but dey done been et up. An' he been a-drinkin' more too. Got to stole dat too."

"Could Bert have *swapped* for any of those things?"

"Miss Liz, ol' Quince'd know if anythang was a-missin' from de place, an' ain't nothin' missin'."

"I don't suppose you've talked to Bert about this, have you?"

"Oh no ma'am. Ain't dis nigger's place to be a-questionin' no white man 'bout sech things."

Liz thought about all this for a minute. "I'll talk to Bert."

"Onliest thing is, Miss Liz, he'll know it uz me put you onto it."

"You're right, Quince. That'll just git you in trouble." Her brow knit. "Then I'll not say anything to Bert. Maybe he'll quit doin' it. I'll talk to you about this again next time I'm over here."

"Thankee, Miss Liz."

Quince should have felt relief at having talked to Miss Liz about the matter, but he didn't. He had a deep foreboding about Mr. Bert's stealing and the direction all of this was going to take.

Chapter 30

The Dallas **Spectator,** October 19, 1864

A shameful problem is the matter of deserters. The area around Denton has become a veritable vipers' nest of this consciousless rabble. Just when our cause is most in need of good men, this spawn of the devil is abandoning duty, honor, and country. May the wrath of a just Creator smite this sorry host.

Two examples to be emulated are General Jerome Robertson, who served with distinction with Hood's Texas Brigade which he commanded until 1863. Since he has returned to Texas where he commands the state's reserve forces. Another is William Harrison Hamman, who was captain of Texas State troops, and is now adjutant general of the Fifth Brigade District with the rank of brigadier general. Hamman enlisted as a private in Hood's Brigade in July, 1861, and served as corporal, then regimental commisary sergeant, then regimental commisary officer. Later he was back in Texas as aide-de-camp to Colonel Likins of the State Troops. These men have not deserted the colors or their responsibilities.

* * *

After the affair with the black brigade they were rushed to defend another fort nearby, which they did successfully in an all-day struggle. Then the front was quiet for a week.

"Thomas, what do you think a soldierin' by now?" Caleb asked.

"Oh, it has its ups and downs. Cain't say much fer the food. No fried chicken, not even on Sundays. My feet and legs is about to git used to the walkin'. And the fellers is all nice. I like Sergeant Ridley fine. And the captain, what's his name, he's alright."

"Captain Rippey. We've had so many captains I cain't hardly keep up with 'em. First there was Captain Sutphin, he signed me up and then brought us up here, then he got sick and went home. Then we had Captain Sealy, boy he didn't care none fer me atall. He got kilt. Then Captain Hamilton, he got kilt in Pennsylvania. He was a purty good feller. And we've had a passel of 'em since. Rippey was here when I come back from Alabama. We been lucky jist to have only two sergeants. I think sergeants is more important to jist the soldiers like us than officers is."

*   *   *

"Form up, men," yelled Sergeant Ridley. "They got us a job a work to do."

The job of work consisted of charging a strong Federal position: log breastworks atop a hill with a swamp and abatis between the Yankees and the Rebels. Lee himself was on hand to direct the action. Caleb happened to be close to Marse Robert when he asked a staff officer what commands were ready. "Only the Texas Brigade is ready, General."

"The Texas Brigade is always ready," was Lee's reply, and Caleb and those others who heard this swelled with pride.

"At least we git to attack fer a change. We been doin' nothin' but defendin' fer a awful long spell."

Thomas replied, "But Caleb, ain't it safer defendin'?"

Heavy Union artillery fire took its toll as they began their charge. They overran an incomplete Northern outwork, but the main work was impossible to take, its defenders firing on the diminished Southerners with new repeating carbines. Among the dead, far in front of the troops, was General Gregg. Caleb, Thomas, and Sergeant Ridley retrieved him in a blanket and carried him to the rear. Later that day Mrs. Gregg came with a wagon to claim the general's body.

*   *   *

Back at the jumping-off point Caleb learned that Jamie had been wounded in the assault. "Where is he at?" Directed to the hospital tent, Caleb was relieved that Jamie was conscious.

"What're you doin' laying around in the middle a the day, boy?"

"Hi, Caleb. Oh, I got a little hole in my side. It ain't bad. Ain't bled much."

"Do it hurt?"

"Some, but I been hurt worser. You 'member that time I fell out of a tree onto that stob and hurt my chest? That hurt a lot worser."

The blood-soaked surgeon assured Caleb that Jamie's wound was not serious. "I hear the brigade is all going into Richmond for General Gregg's funeral. You go ahead on, he's gonna be fine. We'll look after your brother."

* * *

The Reverend Gladson said words over General Gregg. Afterwards Caleb spoke to him. "Those were mighty fine sentiments you spoke over the general, sir."

"Thank you, son. By the way, aren't you the young man I talked to some time ago? I believe you had killed one of our own soldiers because he had a grudge against you and was about to shoot you."

"You sure has a good memory, sir. I'm the one."

"How have things gone for you? Any problems with your conscience since then?"

"No sir. That talk we had done me a world a good, and that's the truth."

"So what has been happening to you since we talked?"

"Well, I got hurt down in Georgia and was away from the army until I got better. By the way, sir, my little brother jist got hurt t'other day, and I'd 'preciate it if maybe you'd say a prayer fer him."

"Is he hurt badly?"

"No sir, it don't look bad atall. But I figger a little prayer or two won't hurt nothin'. 'Specially comin' from a preacher."

"I'd be proud to, my boy."

* * *

Jamie was in high spirits when Caleb and Thomas entered the tent. His color was good and he looked alert.

"Caleb, I thought you tole me this boy had been shot. He looks to me like he's ready to rassle a bear." He shooed a fly away from Jamie's bandaged wound.

Jamie smiled. "I'm feelin' better ever day. Ought to be outa here in a few more days and back with my outfit."

"Are you eatin'?" Caleb asked.

"Well, you know I ain't much of a eater." He ran his hand through his red hair and winced slightly. "What is you boys up to?"

"I don't know if you heerd General Gregg got kilt. We went to his funeral in Richmond," Caleb replied. "Right now we're in the trenches outside a Richmond."

An orderly came up and said, "You need to leave now so he can get some rest."

Thomas said, "You take care, boy. We'll be a-seein' ya."

"Little brother, I'll come back soon as I kin git away. You jist keep on a-gittin' better, you hear?"

"Bye, Caleb. So long, Thomas. I'll be outa here 'fore y'all know it."

*   *   *

Three days later, while Caleb was catching a short nap in the trenches, Sergeant Ridley gently shook him awake. "Caleb, it's yer brother, he's took a turn fer the worst. You better go see him."

Caleb could not believe the change in Jamie. His complexion was gray, he was perspiring heavily although the day was cool, and his breathing was labored. The surgeon was apologetic. "I don't know what happened. He was doing fine, then all of a sudden his fever shot way up yesterday. The only thing I can think of is his wound must have gotten infected."

"Cain't anything be did fer Jamie?"

"We are doing all we can, soldier. But it doesn't look good. That's why we sent for you, just in case he doesn't pull out of this."

"You mean he might die?"

The doctor did not answer. After a pause he left the brothers together.

Caleb knelt beside Jamie's cot. "Jamie, it's Caleb, I'm here."

Jamie opened his eyes; they wore a glaze and were blood-shot. His lips were parched. "Hi, Caleb. It's good to see you, big brother."

"How you feelin'?"

"Not too chipper. I keep feelin' hot and cold."

Caleb took Jamie's hand. "I'm gonna stay right here 'till you git better." And he did, that day and all night and all the next day.

Another soldier came inquiring after Jamie. "Hello, I'm Mike O'Grady."

"Yes, Jamie has mentioned you. Glad you could come."

"How's he doin'?"

"Not too well, Mike. Got a awful high fever."

"Well, I'll be off. Just wanted to look in on the boy-o. Tell him Michael stuck his head in."

"I sure will. Thanks fer comin'."

Jamie's breathing became more exertive, and his fever rose. In his half-sleeps he would mumble and sometimes even whine like a small child. Then he seemed to rally and he looked at Caleb with the clearest eyes of the past several hours. "Caleb, when we git home I'm gonna take ol' Chalkie and we're gonna go down by the crick and he's gonna chase them frogs like he does so funny....And Momma and Poppa and David and Annie and me and you is all gonna climb on the wagon and go into town and see the circus elephant....And we are all gonna laugh and then go home and work in the garden....Caleb, I'm scared. I'm slippin' in....Caleb, don't let me slip in....." His grip on Caleb's hand loosened, and his eyes stared into eternity.

* * *

"Mr. Gladson, I don't unnerstand why he died. He wasn't hurt that bad. He was gittin' better." Caleb's face was tear-stained.

The preacher put his arm around Caleb. "I know you're upset, my boy."

"He wasn't up here hardly no time atall. I been up here a-fightin' fer over three years. How come it wasn't me got kilt 'steada Jamie? It ain't fair."

"It isn't fair. It's never fair for one so young to lose his life. But it was God's will."

"Did you pray fer Jamie, like you tole me you would?"

"Yes I did, son."

"But I don't know how you could of, 'cause I never even tole you his name."

"I asked the Lord to look after the brother of the young man who had killed a fellow soldier in self-defense. He knew who I was referring to."

Caleb shook his head. "I'm sorry sir. I guess I'm jist lookin' fer some reason why Jamie's gone. Lookin' fer somebody to blame. I oughtn't blame you, ner God, ner the doctors, ner myself. I ought to lay the blame where it really belongs, with the Yankees. They's the ones shot 'im."

Back in the line, the brigade was given an urgent call to go to the defense of a small beleaguered force of Virginia home guards, only 20 of them, who were manning a sorely pressed defense line threatened with a Union breakthrough. They moved toward the imperiled point at the double-quick. When the officer commanding the home guards saw the ragged Texans approaching, he threw his hat into the air and shouted, "Glory be to God! We are saved!" The Federal advance was halted. Then a furious counterattack was launched, unordered, spontaneous, led by Caleb, who had the look of a madman as he dashed toward the foe, bayonet fixed and poised to impale the first unlucky Yankee to bar his path.

As the Texan counterattack reached its limit, the men had to restrain Caleb. "Let me go! I wanna keep chargin' them Yankee bastards!" He had to be almost carried back to the Southern lines.

"Damn, Caleb, I never seen you so het up, boy. Was you tryin' to win the war all by yerself?" Sergeant Ridley was obviously proud of his soldier.

Caleb did not reply. He was breathing heavily and seemed preoccupied.

"Pears to me like a good way to git yerself kilt," was Thomas's observation.

Now Caleb was embarrassed. "I hope I didn't look like no show-off."

   *   *   *

A week later, upon the recommendation of Captain Rippey, Caleb was promoted to corporal.

Chapter 31

The Dallas **Spectator,** January 1, 1865

The bold and gallant Hood has seen his army shattered by the apostate Thomas. In a series of actions designed to destroy those Federals left behind by Sherman, Hood has suffered reverses that will be hard to recoup. During this series of campaigns with Hood in Tennessee, Ector's Brigade continued to cover itself in glory, just as it had earlier at Allatoona, Georgia, thus making Texans proud. It was at Allatoona that Brigadier General William Young lost a foot. Ross's Brigade also performed in an outstanding fashion. Brigadier General Hiram Granbury was among many general officers killed, such as Pat Cleburne.

Meanwhile Sherman has continued his march of destruction from Atlanta to the Atlantic, showing the same disregard for civilized behavior as Sheridan has been showing in the Shenandoah Valley. These are truly the times that try men's souls.

Back in Texas is the celebrated John Burke, Lee's "favorite spy". Burke enlisted in Hood's Brigade as a private in early 1861. Shortly he began a career as a scout and spy for Beauregard, Joe Johnston, and "Stonewall"

Jackson. He rode with Jeb Stuart on the famous ride around McClellan's army in 1862. Burke traveled behind Union lines as far as New York. He used disguises, frequently the uniform of a Federal officer, and would even change the color of his artificial eye. His most daring adventure came after he was apprehended in Philadelphia, where he was placed under guard in irons and handcuffs. As the train to Washington crossed a high trestle, Burke jumped into the river and made his way back to Lee. As a colonel he is now adjutant general of Texas.

*   *   *

Jan. 3, 1865
Dear Liz,

I dont have no idee if you will receive this leter but it makes me feel closter to you just to write to you. The winter has been awfull cold in fack we started having frosts way back in sept. We are in huts agin this is my forth winter in the army but I was not with the Brigade last winter I was in Alabama with my aunt Helen and uncle Lawrence. We got the wood for our huts mostly from vacunt houses some of them miles away. We dont hardly have no nales so we have to do the best we can with out them. What we done is we made the framework from the lumber from the houses and used littel logs and saplings for the sides and used mud to chink the sides and also bild a fireplace and a chimly and for the roof we used some canvas and old blankets and tree branchs. We got one side open to the south and its not like home but its beter than being plum out in the open. Wood to burn is hard to find. We spend a lot of time in the trenchs where the Yankee snipers takes shots at us. I gess Thomas must be home by now. When he got shot in the head by that sniper I sure was woried about him I thought he might die like Jamie done. But they said he was well enuf to go home. That scarr on his head sure is ugly. He couldnt see nothing for a day or two.

Gen. Longstreet is back with us in fack has been back sense about Oct. The food is awful scarse sometimes instead of meat we git molasis. Yesterday we was gave a meal by the ladies of Richmond it wasnt much but the mane thing is they thought about us out hear. We do have a good time some, there is a theatr and we sees shows and plays and even 2 wimmin sings and plays for us bout ever night. And we git visters like Mr. Reagan from Tex. He is the post master I ast him about the mail and he says some gits by and some don't. Also Mr Lubbock who was gov. of Texas he is on Jeff Davis staff. Also mr. Wigfall he use to be over us & now he is a Senter, the boys dont care much for him becaus he didnt want Gen. Hood to be over the army of Tenesse but Gen Hood he got it anyways.

There is more fellers goin to church meetins than I every seen before. We has lost so many boys that may hav somthing to do with it, also their aint a lot to do, the fightin' is slo. Myself I havnt gone to church no more than before. I sure do miss Jamie.

I dont know if you know I am a corporal now. We captured a mess of prisners some white and some colored, by the way tell Quince I say hello.

I have been writting about me but what about you. Hope you all had a good crop of cotton and a good

Christmas and all of you are well. I miss you girl and love you and want to see you. I hope soon.
Love
Caleb
P. S. There is so few of us that we dont need as many huts as we use to. I am with some boys that was in anuther company one of them is Mike who was Jamies frend.

*   *   *

In the trenches there was little fighting and virtually no movement by the brigade. Rumors flew: the entire brigade was to be returned to Texas to replenish its depleted ranks by recruiting; the brigade was to be merged with other units, thus losing its separate identity. This last met with stout resistance. A delegation was sent to President Davis to protest the coalition of the Texas Brigade with other commands. Lee himself helped prevent the merger by saying to Mr. Davis, "Before you decide let me say that I never ordered the Texans to hold a place that they did not hold it." The president let the brigade stay separate, although its strength was down to under 600 effectives.

In late January, in a mass meeting, the brigade passed resolutions of loyalty to the Confederacy. Early the following month nine gold stars representing heroism were passed out by the unpopular Wigfall; Caleb received one of them.

Chapter 32

▼

The Dallas **Spectator,** March 30, 1865

Matters have seldom looked worse for our cause. The Valley is lost, Petersburg and Richmond are being strangled as the railroads are being cut, Charleston has been lost, and Johnston who replaced Hood has been defeated at Bentonville, North Carolina.

However, had it not been for Terry's Texas Rangers, commanded by the senior regimental officer on the field, Lieutenant James Mathews, the entire army would have been surrounded. Mathews was asked by General Hardee to hold a bridge, and it was done.

Colonel Sul Ross is back in Texas to recruit for his depleted brigade. We have learned that General William Whiting has died a prisoner in New York. He was one of the finest engineers in Confederate service. He had been wounded and captured at Fort Fisher. Whiting had done much worthwhile work in Texas before the war, including laying out roads and helping clear the Colorado River raft. He will be sorely missed.

* * *

On a spring night the Texas Brigade was ordered out of the trenches around Richmond and put on trains for Petersburg. It was evident that the Army of Northern Virginia was abandoning the capital to the Federals after four years of intense, gallant, brilliant defense. The men were sad. Some cried, many cursed. Caleb was philosophical. "I s'pect General Lee figgers we cain't hold it no more. Jist too many Yankees, too few a us."

They were shocked to learn that the Petersburg defenses too were being relinquished. "Sergeant Ridley, what does you make a this?"

"Pears like the army is pullin' out so we kin do some maneuverin', that's what General Lee is at his best at anyhow, bein' able to move around and hit the Yankees where they least expects it. Also we got to git somethin' to eat somewheres, there ain't none in Richmond *or* Petersburg, and we're 'bout starvin' to death."

"Amen to that," said Caleb. "My clothes is fallin' off me. I'm afeared my ribs is gonna poke through my skin."

Lee designated the Texans as the rear guard in the evacuation of Petersburg. "Quite a honor fer us, boys," announced the sergeant. They left the city in flames.

They marched to the west with no food and little rest. Repeatedly they had to form defense lines to parry the probing thrusts of Union cavalry and sometimes even infantry. They moved like shadows in a dream, doing everything automatically, without thinking, almost without orders. They complained little, knowing it would do no good. Their officers urged them on, assuring them that food and rest were to be had ahead, but they must keep moving.

Long lines of Federal infantry and cavalry could be seen in the distance, shadowing them. They had not seen so many Yankees since their perch on the heights at Fredericksburg, over two years earlier. "Wonder if them Yankees is as tired and hungry as we is?"

"Are you kiddin'? They're as fat and sassy as hogs in the fall, right before slaughterin'," replied the sergeant.

Many of the discouraged Southerners were throwing their equipment down, either out of fatigue or hopelessness. Some even dropped their muskets. Desertion was becoming commonplace.

Caleb observed an officer feeding dried corn to his horse. Some of the kernels fell to the ground; as soon as the officer departed, Caleb watched men search the dust for the kernels, blow on them, and devour them. "I'm hungry, God knows, but I ain't *that* hungry."

After a week of retreating, hunger, weariness, word came down the line that Lee had surrendered the army. At first there was widespread disbelief, but as the news was deemed official the men wept, swore, or simply shook their heads. There was more sadness than relief. Many men smashed or bent their pieces so the Northerners couldn't use them. "I wouldn't do that, boys," Sergeant Ridley advised them. "If yer guns is damaged you may not be paroled." With this information there was a frantic effort to restore muskets to their former condition.

Caleb heard a man say, "I'd ruther have died than surrender, but if Marse Bob thinks that is best, then all I have got to say is that Marse Bob has got to be right as usual." Caleb thought, I agree with the part about Marse Bob but not the part about dyin'. I'm gonna be a livin' man! The realization that the war was over and he had survived was like a physical shock. He laughed out loud. He began to shake the hand of every man he could. They thought he was daft, and many were angry. "Boy, why you celebratin' us losin'?"

"I ain't celebratin' us *losing*, I'm celebratin' us *livin*'!"

Now he would see his folks, the farm. Now he would see Liz, marry her if he was lucky. Be a father. Live to be an old man like his Poppa. He felt reborn.

And then another thought hit him: Quince would be a free man!

*   *   *

Next morning they were formed up and read Lee's farewell address, which brought tears to the eyes of virtually every man. Then they returned to their pitiful campsite and were issued Federal rations, their first real meal in weeks. A few of the men ate so much so fast that they became ill. But it was a happy kind of ill.

*   *   *

It had been raining almost continually since the day of the surrender three days before, as if all nature were sad that their cause had been lost. Now it was time to stack their guns and surrender their flags. They marched between lines of Yankees, who were well-dressed and fat compared to the scarecrow appearance of the Southerners. Occasionally there was a sneer or a caustic remark from the victors, but mostly they were as subdued as the vanquished. Caleb thought that they too were glad the killing was over, and they could go to their homes in the North and resume *their* interrupted lives. Then a startling thing happened. The Union general in charge of the surrender, Chamberlain, ordered his men to salute their ragged vanquished foe. Most of the Southerners would never forget this gracious act of magnanimity.

*   *   *

They passed by the provost marshal tables and picked up their paroles. Now it was time to go home.

Chapter 33

The Dallas **Spectator,** April 20, 1865

General Lee has surrendered the heroic Army of Northern Virginia, but other Confederate armies are still in the field. However with the surrender of Lee, recently elevated to command of all our armies, the situation is bleak.

President Lincoln has been assassinated, and been replaced by Andrew Johnson of Tennessee. Whether the accession to power of this Southerner bodes well or ill for our section remains to be discovered.

Among those surrendered by General Lee at Appomattox Court House, Virginia, was the famed Texas Brigade, by all accounts the finest fighting unit in the Southern armies, though much depleted. The men have been paroled, and according to the terms of their paroles, are not supposed to join any other fighting units. So we may expect them to be coming home shortly. If ever there were heroes, if ever a fight was well fought, Hood's Brigade more than qualifies.

* * *

In 1861 Caleb had come to Virginia on a train. Now it was 1865 and the Southern railroad network had been destroyed by Yankees and by hard use. So he would have to walk.

His companion was Mike O'Grady, Jamie's friend and later his as well, bound for Galveston. Caleb liked the chunky Irishman because he was steady, resourceful, loquacious, never moody, never down. He like Caleb was mostly happy to be alive. In their weeks together they talked frequently about how they both detested human bondage.

"It's degradin'. Both to the master and the servant. Puts me in mind of the bloody English with their boots on the necks of the Irish."

"Then why did you fight fer the South, Mike?"

"Didn't have no choice, boy-o. Was conscripted."

"Like Thomas. Hope he made it home alright."

"How's come you to be in the army, Caleb, if you hate slavery so?"

Caleb was thoughtful for a long while. Finally he said, "Michael, I don't really know. I guess I didn't want to look like no coward in front a my little brother ner my Poppa."

As they walked through North Carolina and Georgia the weather got warmer and the countryside more verdant. They heard more birds singing and saw more squirrels, rabbits (Caleb recollected "Danny), even an occasional fox or deer. The people along the way were mostly kind and generous, feeding them outright or letting them earn meals by doing chores. Sometimes they encountered hostility. "How come you boys let the damn

Yankees whup you? Ain't no way a Yankee ought to beat a Southern boy."

When they replied at all it was usually to the effect that there were just too many of the foe.

When they reached Montgomery, Alabama, and a group of them were required to unload a transport filled with Union supplies before they themselves could be loaded for the river trip to Mobile, they were flabbergasted by the wealth of goods at the North's disposal: food, uniforms, tents, guns, ammunition—all the necessities of war which they had never had enough of. Caleb cried, "Boys, we could of never whupped the Yankees. They jist simply had too much of everthing we lacked. Plus the *numbers* of 'em. How did we do as well as we done?"

From Mobile they took steamer to New Orleans. Caleb recalled how the women of New Orleans had been so generous with clothing when the "Texicans" had arrived so ill-clad from their wet walk across Louisiana. He learned that the same magnanimous spirit still prevailed, as the women of the city found clothing for the ragged Texans once again. Caleb thought the second time the more remarkable. "Mike, when we come through here back in '61 we was heroes because as fer as these folks knew we was goin' up and whup the Yankees. This time *we* was the ones had been whupped, and the ladies *still* give clothes. Now *that* is *real* generosity."

From New Orleans they went by ship to Galveston, where Caleb bade Mike an affectionate farewell. "You take care a yerself, you hear? Reckon you kin git yer old job back loadin' and unloadin' ships?"

"There's always a job fer a man with a strong back and weak mind sich as Oi've got. Caleb, all the best to ya. Have a long life, boy-o."

*   *   *

On the long walk alone to North Texas Caleb had much time to reflect and to wonder. Why had he lived when so many had died? Good God, how many were there? Ben Sammons. Pat. Wash. Tolly. John the Baptist. Eli. Tom. Ben Larkin. Bill. Sergeant Trammell. Henry. Aaron. Captain Sealy. Captain Hamilton. "Stonewall" Jackson. General Gregg. And Jamie. It was almost too depressing to recall all of them.

But on the other hand he was glad he had got to know them. If there had been no war, his path and those of his companions would never have crossed. Except of course Jamie.

He was honored to have served under General Lee. And General Longstreet. And especially General Hood. Too bad that Hood had lost his entire army in Tennessee. Maybe he had been moved *too* high. Maybe he was cut out to command just a brigade, maybe a whole division. But apparently one had to be truly special, like Lee, to run a whole army. And even Marse Robert had lost.

And what about Liz? Would she be as glad to see him as he would to see her? Had she something going with Bert? Soon he would know.

At least Quince would be a free man. Caleb wondered what Quince would do. Where would he live? Would he have his own farm or would he work for someone else?

With Jamie gone, would he work for us? Soon he would know that too.

Chapter 34

The Dallas **Spectator,** July 4, 1865

The war is lost! Every Confederate command has now surrendered: Joe Johnston in North Carolina, Bedford Forrest and Dick Taylor in Alabama, and finally our own commanding general of the Trans-Mississippi Department, Kirby Smith, in New Orleans.

Only time will answer these compelling questions: How could we have not prevailed? What will become of us at the hands of the Federals? Will they be magnanimous, or will they be vengeful?

Our gallant men are returning, looking for the most part like scarecrows. How did they all do as well as they did? For as long as they did? We must be forever grateful for their effort, their bravery, their sacrifice.

And so many men are not returning, not now, not ever. They have given the last full measure of devotion.

*   *   *

When Caleb came to the place where the road led to the Sammons place he hesitated. Should he go inquire about Quince? He decided against it, telling himself he ought to see his own folks first. But there was also the tiny nagging fear that he might find Liz there.

When his house came into view his pace quickened. Everything looked about as he remembered them: rain barrel under the left corner eave, his Momma's washpot upside down by the back stoop, the well with the bucket hoisted above it, the outhouse, the barn with its adjoining fences for the stock, the chicken coops, the plow. Now down the road came Chalkie, barking at him as if he were an intruder. Chalkie stopped ten feet away and Caleb called his name. The dog hesitated, then tentatively approached Caleb. As the almost-forgotten scent was recognized Chalkie went into a frenzy of jumping and licking, as if to make up for four years of his young master's absence. The two of them happily proceeded toward the house.

Caleb's mother came out the back door, wiping her hands on her apron. She embraced her son and began to cry softly. "Is Jamie with you, boy?"

"No'm."

"Did he git hurt?"

"Yes'm, Momma."

"Hurt bad?"

"Yes'm. Jamie's dead."

Then they both cried.

"Yer Poppa's out in the field. Annie and David is both a-helpin' 'im. They oughta be in fer dinner in a little while." They went into the house and Caleb dropped his meager belongings in a corner. "How did Jamie die? Was you with him?"

"Yes'm, I was. He got shot, but not bad. Everbody thought he was gonna be alright. But then he took a bad turn...." It was hard to tell his mother about the death of his little brother.

She embraced him. "I jist thank the good Lord *you're* back safe. And I'm thankful you was with him and he didn't die all alone."

After an interval he asked, "Do you know anything about the Wrights? About Elizabeth?"

"As a matter of fack she was jist over here yestiddy."

Caleb hardly knew how to proceed. "Did she say anything about me?"

"Said she still ain't heard from you. She wrote you all the time 'til she learned the war was lost. Then she figgered you'd be a-comin' home lessen you'd been kilt. Or lessen you decided to stay in Virginia fer one reason or 'nother."

Caleb took this as hopeful news and decided not to question his mother further. He would go see Liz, and soon.

   *   *   *

The reunion with his father, brother, and sister was warm, accompanied by Caleb's amazement at how his siblings had grown and changed. Their amazement was mostly about how skinny and bronzed *he* was. "You look like you've saw a lotta livin', boy," was his father's observation.

"I surely have, Poppa, and a lotta dyin'. All I ever wanta see a dyin' the rest a my life."

"So it was bad?"

"Yessir. It was bad."

His mother killed two chickens for supper. "So glad to have my boy home safe after all these years." He ate heartily but hastily, hoping his folks wouldn't be too upset by his deteriorated table manners. For he had one more call to make before dark.

*   *   *

The Wright place was quiet. He walked onto the porch and knocked on the post. It was Mr. Wright who answered. "Caleb? I'll swan, it is you, boy! Come in this house!"

Inside was Mrs. Wright and Rachel, now fourteen. "Rachel, I sure wouldn't have knew you if'n I hadn't saw you in yer own house. You're mighty growed up and purty."

Rachel blushed and barely audibly uttered a shy "Thank you". Then she and her mother continued preparing their meal.

Mr. Wright offered, "Lizzie is milkin' down to the barn. 'Spect she'll be glad to see you, boy."

"Thank you, Mr. Wright. Is it alright if I jist go on down and supprise 'er?"

Assured it was alright, Caleb headed for the barn. Again a hopeful sign: "Spect she'll be glad to see you." His heart was racing by the time he entered the barn, in time to see Liz getting up from the milking stool and removing the bucket from under the cow. Caleb thought that Liz had achieved a maturity and a character that, in concert with her tanned skin, white teeth, brown eyes, and dark ringlets, made her more beautiful than ever.

When she saw him she dropped the milk bucket. "Caleb!" She threw herself into his arms and squeezed him so hard he could scarcely breathe. Then she kissed him with four years' worth of passion. "Oh Caleb! I am so glad to see you. I didn't know if you was alive or dead. You're so skinny, boy! Didn't they feed you nothin'?"

He did not reply, but just alternated between kissing her, looking at her lovely face, and hugging her. After five minutes they sat on a bale of hay, holding hands, and had a conversation.

"I guess Thomas got home alright."

"Yes, but he ain't in very good shape. Has blackouts all the time. Can't hardly work on their farm. Margaret is afraid they might lose their place. Neighbors has been helpin' some but they got their own troubles."

"Did Thomas tell you I was alright?"

"From talkin' to Thomas you couldn't tell nothin'. He's just real confused. Has nightmares. You wouldn't believe the scar on his head."

"Yes I would. I seen it right after he was hit by that sniper. I s'pose it's a wonder he got home."

"Speakin' of gittin' home, I thought you just might not come home."

"What do you mean, Liz?"

"I thought you might just stay there in Virginia with Mary."

Caleb had to think about this for awhile. "Mary? You mean Mary Tolbert?"

"I don't know her last name. All I know is you seemed to think highly of her. Said she was like a angel."

Caleb laughed "Why, I'd nearly fergot about her. That was so long ago. I doubt I ever saw her more'n two or three times. Did you think there was somethin' serious goin' on between me and Mary?"

"Well, you never wrote me again after the letter about her, so what was I s'posed to think?"

"Never wrote to you? Why, I must of wrote you twenny letters after that one."

"Well, I never got none of 'em."

He cleared his throat. "The last letter I got from you sounded like maybe you and Bert Sammons had somethin' sparkin'."

"Bert Sammons? Caleb, you got to be funnin' me. Bert? Why, I hate Bert Sammons. Yes, I felt sorry for him there for a little while when he first come back from the war with a hand missin', but Mr. Bert fixed that awful quick. Me and Bert? That's the silliest, craziest, foolishest thing I ever heard, boy."

"Well, I quit a-hearin' from you about that time."

"That ain't because I quit *writin'*, 'cause I must of wrote you twenny or thirty letters after the one about Bert. Somebody said not much mail was gittin' through between here and Virginia because the Yankees was all along the Missippi."

"That's what I figger too. We was both a-writin' but none of it was reachin' the other one. What about Quince? I s'pose he's a free man now."

Her bright visage darkened. "You ain't heard then?"

"Heard what?"

"Quince is dead."

Caleb was stunned. "Dead? How come?"

"Bunch of white people killed him."

"Why? Because they didn't want him to be a free man?"

"Didn't have nothin' to do with that, Caleb. They thought he'd been stealin'."

"That's crazy. Quince wouldn't steal nothin'."

"I know that. It was Bert had been a-stealin'. Quince and me talked about it. Bert had been takin' stock and liquor from folks around here. Then he broke into the store and stole some guns. A kinda posse got on the trail and it led to the Sammons place. They just assumed it was Quince took the guns, 'specially since Bert had hid 'em in Quince's room when he was workin'. They hung 'im right there on the place."

"Didn't Bert say nothin'? Didn't Quince tell 'em he didn't do it?"

"Quince tried but you know they ain't gonna believe a nigger. And I think some of 'em was bitter we lost the war and slavery was over. As fer Bert, he was conveniently not there."

"What about ol' Mr. Sammons?"

"He's too old, and his back is all stove up, and besides, nobody never asked him. They just hung Quince." She teared up. "I wish I'd been there or knew about it. Maybe I coulda saved poor Quince. He was such a good man."

"Now don't be blamin' yerself, Liz. Wasn't nothin' you could of did. That's jist a real shame."

They were both sad about Quince, but their youth and their intense happiness of seeing each other and relief that the other was unencumbered soon changed their mood back to cheerful. "Let's take a walk." By now it was dark, and they made their way hand in hand to the big oak tree, under whose branches they soon made love in their accustomed way.

Epilogue

In 1872 Hood's Texas Brigade Association held its reunion in Houston, and the newspapers announced that John B. Hood himself was scheduled to attend.

"Liz, I'd sure like to go. Do you think you could spare me fer a few days?"

"Of course, goose. You're not that precious," she smiled.

"I could go down on the railroad. It's up to Dallas now."

So he went. On the train Caleb thought he recognized the conductor.

"Was you in the Texas Brigade?"

"Why yes. Then I was captured in Tennessee and spent the rest of the war in a Federal prison camp in Illinois. My name is Lawrence Daffan."

"I'm Caleb Walker. I was wounded in the leg in Tennessee at Chickamauga, same as General Hood. In fact, that's where I'm headed, to the Brigade's reunion."

"Wish I could go, but I've gotta work. Tell them I said howdy."

"I sure will, Mr. Daffan."

Among hundreds in attendance Caleb recognized many, including Sergeant Ridley, and they reminisced longingly of the old days in Virginia and Maryland and Pennsylvania and Georgia and Tennessee.

He also saw Captain Barziza who had gone down at Gettysburg and been picked up by Yankees. "I thought maybe you was dead, sir."

"No, just badly hurt. I spent a year in federal hospitals, then some time at a prison camp in Maryland. They were sending me by train to another prison camp in Pennsylvania, but I dove out an open window and escaped to Canada."

But it was General Hood that Caleb had come all this way to see. The great man, his left arm still in a sling, was surrounded by admirers for hours at a time, but Caleb was patient. When he was finally able to make his way up to Hood, he looked up into the sad eyes and said, "General Hood, I don't expect you remember me, but I'm Caleb Walker. I come to see you when we was both in the hospital in Atlanta after your leg was took off at Chickamauga."

Hood smiled faintly and extended his large hand. "Of course I remember you, soldier. It meant a great deal to me that you came. How have you been? How is your wound?"

"Oh, it got okay real fast. I went on back up to Virginia that next spring. How have you been, sir?"

"Very well indeed. I'm living in New Orleans now. Have business interests there. I'm married and have a large family."

"That's jist great, general. I sure do remember New Orleans. Went through there goin' to the war and a-comin' back. Looks like yer new leg is a-doin' fine."

"I've got so used to it I hardly remember I wasn't born with it. Do you have a family, son?"

"Yessir. My wife Elizabeth and me has two young'uns."

"That's very nice, soldier. What are their names?"

"Well sir, we named our little girl Virginia, since I spent so much time up there. And last winter Liz had a little boy. We called him Hood Lee Walker."

There were tears in their eyes as they parted for the last time.

Printed in the United States
50148LVS00003B/80